8

89

89

89

92

4

1997

BOOKS BY KRISTI D. HOLL

Just Like a Real Family
Mystery By Mail   *(Escapade)*
Footprints Up My Back

FOOTPRINTS
UP MY BACK

FOOTPRINTS UP MY BACK

~◊~

Kristi D. Holl

Atheneum/1984/New York

LIBRARY OF CONGRESS CATALOGING IN PUBLICATION DATA
Holl, Kristi D.
Footprints up my back.
Summary: With the help of her grandmother, good-natured,
dependable Jean finally realizes that only she can prevent
other people from taking advantage of her.
[1. Self-assertion—Fiction. 2. Behavior—Fiction.
3. Family life—Fiction] I. Title.
PZ7.H7079Fo 1984   [Fic]   84-4168
ISBN 0-689-31070-6

Published simultaneously in Canada by
McClelland & Stewart, Ltd.
Composition by Maryland Linotype Composition Company
Baltimore, Maryland
Printed and bound by Fairfield Graphics
Fairfield, Pennsylvania
Designed by Christine Kettner
First Edition

To Jenny

Contents

FOOTPRINTS UP MY BACK

1

Being Dependable
Is a Curse!

Plastic plates whizzed through the air as twelve-year-old Jean Harvey set the supper table. Silverware clattered as she dropped knives and forks beside each plate. Jean couldn't believe she was stuck with Belinda's chores again.

At the kitchen sink, Jean ran a large saucepan full of hot water. She fumed as she stared out the window at the fading spring sunset. She didn't mind doing Belinda's chores once in a while. But this was the third time that week her older sister hadn't shown up to fix supper.

Both of their parents worked and didn't get home until six o'clock. Jean and her fifteen-year-old sister took turns cooking supper. Although this was supposed to be Belinda's week to cook, Jean was left with the job again.

She banged the pan of water down on the stove, slopping some over the side. She had looked forward all day to going swimming at the Y with Stacy Michaels. They had planned to go right after school.

But four o'clock came. Then four-thirty. Then four-forty-five. Jean had given up watching for Belinda at the window. It didn't really matter by then. It was already too late for her to go swimming and be home in time for supper.

Swallowing her disappointment, Jean had called Stacy and said she couldn't go after all. It wasn't just that supper had to be cooked. Her six-year-old brother Mark wasn't supposed to be left alone in the house.

Gradually Jean's anger faded as she molded the hamburger into patties. She wished she had the nerve to refuse to bail out her sister. She should just let her get in trouble. But Jean hated it when everyone was mad at each other. It tied her stomach up in knots. For some reason, her parents seemed to count on her to see that things ran smoothly at home. They always called her their sensible middle child.

"Being dependable is a curse," Jean mumbled as the water began to boil.

She poured macaroni from two boxes into the boiling water. Giving it a quick stir, she got out the butter, milk and cheese. While cutting the cheese into cubes, she wondered if Stacy had invited some-one else to go swimming that night.

A key turning in the back door brought Jean out of her thoughts. She hastily flipped the browning hamburgers, then stirred the macaroni.

Marge and Dan Harvey, laughing at something Jean couldn't hear, came into the kitchen.

Kicking off her shoes, Jean's mother sniffed. "Something smells good." She peered in the pans on the stove and hugged Jean at the same time. "I thought Belinda was cooking this week."

Jean's father, the manager of a lumberyard, brushed sawdust from his pants legs. "Don't tell me Belinda isn't home yet! Something's going to have to be done about her, Marge."

"She just loses track of time," her mother ex-plained. "I was the same way at her age. At least Jean is always here to take over."

Resentment flared in Jean. Her mother assumed that she had nothing better to do than fill in for her sister. No one in the family seemed to think that Jean might have plans of her own.

Her father scrubbed his hands at the sink. "But Belinda is three years older. Why can't she be as dependable as Jean is?"

Jean sighed, having heard this conversation many times. Belinda got her parents' attention even when she wasn't there. Jean often felt that no one even noticed *her*. But one thing was sure. Since her family couldn't afford a maid, they would always need her around.

The front door opened and slammed shut. Jean continued tearing up salad greens. Five seconds later Belinda stuck her head through the kitchen door.

"Thank heavens you fixed supper, Jean!" Her breath came in gasps. "I was studying with Jolene when I saw what time it was. I ran all the way home from the library."

Jean swallowed the angry words that came to her lips. "That's okay, I guess," she mumbled. Only it wasn't. After supper, upstairs in their bedroom, Jean intended to tell her so.

Their father poured milk into the glasses on the table. "It would be nice if you'd call, Belinda. You'd save us a lot of worry."

"I'm sorry, Dad. Really." Belinda kissed her father on the cheek. "I'll try to do better. Honest."

Jean watched her father's frown disappear. She rolled her eyes toward the ceiling. Her father simply couldn't be strict with Belinda. In fact, no one stayed mad at her very long.

"Come to the table," Jean called. She set the hamburgers, macaroni and cheese and salad on the table. "Time to eat!"

Her mother padded into the kitchen. She'd changed from her dress and high heels to baggy slacks and house slippers.

Mark followed close behind her, his untied shoelaces slapping the tiled floor. He crawled onto his chair, pushed the salad bowl away from him and knocked over his glass of milk.

"Slorruy." His words were garbled by the giant grape sour ball in his mouth.

His mother sighed and mopped up the milk. "Mark, take that candy out of your mouth."

Belinda dropped her books on the counter with a thud. Jean joined her parents at the table, but Belinda halted abruptly.

"Good grief! I can't eat that heavy food. There's a million calories there!" She rummaged in the refrigerator. Bringing a carton of low fat yogurt with her, she gracefully slid into her chair.

Jean smiled to herself. Belinda was always trying to lose weight, although Jean could never understand why. On the other hand, Jean reflected, her mother could stand to lose fifteen pounds. But her mom often said that life was too short to worry about her weight.

"Belinda, don't you think you should eat more than that?" Her mother eyed the yogurt doubtfully. "You're still a growing girl."

"But I'm growing in the wrong direction—out!" Belinda dug into her plain yogurt. "Anyway, that meat is full of cholesterol that clogs your arteries, and all the starch in the macaroni! Ugh!" She shuddered dramatically.

Her jaw clenched, Jean scooped an extra large spoonful of macaroni and cheese onto her plate. At least *she* liked the meal she had cooked. It was bad enough that Belinda couldn't show up to fix supper without making cracks about it.

"What's wrong with eating a little salad?" her mother coaxed Belinda. "Surely there's nothing fattening about that."

Belinda gasped. "But mother! Don't you know they grow all these vegetables using pesticides and poisons and—"

"Enough, enough!" Their father made a slicing motion with a finger across his throat. "Let a hard-working man enjoy his meal without hearing about clogged arteries and pesticides."

As her father changed the topic to the new wood paneling at the lumberyard, Jean stopped listening. She knew all about woodwork—she disappeared into it all the time. Jean admitted to herself that Belinda was impossible to ignore. But it would have been nice if *someone* had asked how *her* day had gone.

Suddenly Jean brightened. At least Belinda would do the dishes after supper. Maybe she and Stacy could go swimming after all.

Jean loved to swim, especially practicing head stands and other stunts in the water. Sometimes she dreamed of working in a professional water show. Jean knew she'd love to wear glittering costumes, swim under colored lights to pulsating music . . .

Her mother broke into her thoughts. "Thanks for fixing supper, Jean." She pushed back her chair. "I have to run over to Grandma's. I bought some

dress material for her today. I'll be right back."
Grandma Harvey lived only four blocks away. Jean's
mother often ran errands for her on her lunch hour.

"Want me to go too?" Jean's father asked.

"No, thanks. I know there's a ball game on TV
tonight you want to see. I won't be gone long." She
pulled on a jacket and waved as she closed the back
door.

Jean's dad ruffled Mark's blond hair as they headed
for the living room. Soon the sports announcer's
squawking voice filled the house.

"I'm late. I've got to go too," Belinda said, patting
her strawberry-blond curls. She threw away her
yogurt carton and started for the door.

"Hey! Where are you going?" Jean's voice rose
to a squeak.

Belinda turned, an arched eyebrow raised. "It's
Friday night. Jackie's picking me up in ten minutes
to go shopping."

"Oh, no, you don't!" Jean pointed an accusing
finger at her sister. "I'm not getting stuck with the
dishes too."

"You really don't mind, do you?" Belinda asked,
sounding puzzled. "After all, what plans could a
twelve-year-old have for a Friday night?"

"Well, nothing definite—"

"You see?" Belinda glided over to Jean and put
her arm around her shoulders. "I know. What if I
lend you my new pink and white belt? You can wear

it to school on Monday." A wheedling note crept into her voice. "I'd really be grateful if you did the dishes tonight."

Jean chewed her bottom lip. It was hard to say "no" to Belinda when she acted so sweet and sincere. It was only in the last year or so that Belinda had seemed so selfish and flighty. Before that, Jean really loved Belinda and felt closer to her. Why did things change? Why couldn't Belinda care about *her*?

A honk sounded outside. "That's probably Jackie." Belinda spoke softly. "What shall I tell her?"

Sighing, Jean finally nodded. "Go ahead," she mumbled.

"Thanks!" Belinda dashed to the front door, slamming it behind her.

Jean began running hot water in the sink. Squirting in a stream of dish soap, she swirled her fingers aimlessly in the water to stir up some suds.

Jean scowled as she scraped the stuck-on macaroni in the bottom of the saucepan. She'd just about had it with her family. She didn't intend to spend the rest of her life in the kitchen, boiling macaroni. . . .

Someday she would be dunking live lobsters in boiling water instead. She'd be . . . a famous international chef, working in an elegant restaurant in Paris. Although she'd cooked before the crowned heads of Europe, she would have never forgotten her humble beginnings in Goldridge.

Hands dangling in the dishwater, Jean smiled slowly . . . Someday, assistant cooks would scramble around a spotless French kitchen. They'd consider it a great honor to watch master chef Jean Harvey creating intricate dishes.

While she worked a timid knock would come at the kitchen door. Before finishing her chocolate soufflé, Jean would pause, her spatula in the air. A cook's helper opened the door to four common beggars. Jean, after a glance in their direction, would continue her delicate mixing and folding.

"Jean! Don't you recognize us?" cried a desperate voice.

Jean whirled to face the beggars, her spotless chef's hat tilting forward. "Belinda . . . *you?*" she asked in amazement.

The bedraggled figure nodded, then hung her head in shame. Studying the other thin faces, Jean recognized her mother, father and Mark. They were gaunt—it looked as if they hadn't eaten in weeks.

Jean knew they had brought their wretched poverty on themselves, but she could not harden her heart toward them. She generously forgave their mistakes, ordering her assistants to spread her family a feast. Their gratitude showed plainly in their sad eyes, which were brimming with tears. . . .

Water spilling over onto the counter jerked Jean out of her daydream. Quickly she turned off the faucets and mopped up the soapy water.

Half an hour later Jean had finished washing and stacking the supper dishes. She decided to try to get her homework done that night. Then maybe on

Saturday she and Stacy could have some fun. She spread her math book and papers out across her twin bed.

"Jean! Are you in your room?" her mother called. "I'm in the bathroom sorting laundry."

Jean had heard her come home a few minutes earlier. "I'm doing my math," she called back.

"Can you please run this load of laundry downstairs for me? Set the water temperature on hot."

Slamming her book shut, Jean stomped across her bedroom. She really didn't mind doing her share of the work. But she was always the first person her family asked when they wanted a chore done.

Her mother looked up from turning socks right side out. "What would I do without you, Jean?" her mother said. "You're such a help to me."

Jean smiled halfheartedly. "Just this load here?" she asked, pointing to a red basket full of towels.

She picked up the load and clomped down the stairs to the kitchen, then down another flight of stairs to the cool basement. Loading the machine, she remembered why Belinda didn't run the washer anymore.

The last time she'd used it, Belinda had dyed her bed sheets purple plum. But she'd forgotten to rinse the washer out afterwards. The next load—her father's underwear—had turned a sickly lavender.

She added soap and put the lid down, then cleaned out the dryer's lint trap. Taking the stairs two at a time, Jean heard her father and brother shouting at the baseball players on TV.

As she passed the living room, her father glanced at her. "While you're up, Jean, could you get us some peanuts? We're really working up an appetite!" He clapped Mark on the back. "Aren't we, sport?"

"Schlure are," Mark said, drooling around his sour ball.

Pivoting on her heel, Jean backtracked to the kitchen. Pouring salted peanuts in a bowl, she chewed her bottom lip. Her family didn't really need another daughter, she decided. As long as they had a servant, they probably wouldn't miss her at all.

Setting the bowl of peanuts on the living room table, Jean noticed the evening newspaper. On the front of the Goldridge *Times* was a picture of an adorable puppy. Under the photograph the caption read: "Looking for a Good Home."

Jean skimmed the article, then reread it carefully. The Goldridge Animal Shelter was making a plea for more families to give an animal a home. A fifteen-dollar service fee would release any dog for adoption, including the puppy in the picture.

Jean tore the picture and article from the paper and carried it back to her room. She flopped on her back on her bed, staring at the picture of the puppy.

I wish I could bring him home, she thought wistfully. But she knew he might as well cost a hundred and fifty dollars as fifteen dollars. Still, a pet of her own would be wonderful. A puppy would love her just for herself, not because she was handy to have around.

And that, Jean decided, would be a really welcome change.

2

Beware Of Borrowers

After a boring weekend, Jean was glad to get back
to school on Monday. Students chattered in small
groups around the sixth grade room. The teacher,
Miss Brookner, stood at the back window.

Jean spotted Stacy feeding the class's hamsters.
Joining her, she apologized again for canceling their
swim on Friday.

Stacy shrugged. "Too bad you couldn't come. The
Silver Sharks were practicing, so I watched for a
while." She filled the hamsters' water container,
then closed the little wire door. "You swim as well
as any of them."

Secretly Jean thought so too. "Wish I could have
seen them practicing. Their shows are sensational.
When's their next performance?"

Stacy plopped down in her seat, her fuzzy pigtails bouncing. "Their spring show is sometime in May."

The Six Silver Sharks were six girls from Miss Brookner's and Mr. Thompson's sixth grades. They had formed a synchronized swimming group two years ago. Jean loved their shiny silver costumes with fins on the back. The fins glittered as the girls sliced through the rippling water. The group gave three performances at the Y, in the fall, winter and spring. Jean felt that to be a Silver Shark was the highest honor any sixth-grade girl could win.

Sometimes, when Jean swam alone, she glided through the chlorinated pool, twisting and diving in rhythm. In her mind she heard the swell of music over loudspeakers. She imagined rainbow-colored lights dancing on the water. She had never confided in anyone, not even Stacy, but she would have given anything to be a Silver Shark.

Miss Brookner bustled to the front of the room and flicked the lights on and off. The small groups of students broke apart. With a small wave, Jean wandered to her desk.

The morning passed quickly as Jean outlined her book report for English. She completed her assignment before the others and laid her paper on Miss Brookner's desk. Jean loved finishing early because they were allowed to go to the library for the rest of the English period.

Miss Brookner motioned for her to wait. "If you wouldn't mind, Jean, I have some math quizzes I'd like you to check. I want to hand them out before lunch today."

Jean's shoulders sagged. She had corrected papers before and usually enjoyed it. But today she wanted to go to the library. That morning Stacy had returned a new mystery. Jean wanted to check it out before anyone else did.

She picked up the stack of quizzes and the answer key. Taking them back to her desk, she dutifully checked each problem. At least she got to use the teacher's red felt pen. It gave her a real feeling of power when she made slashing red check marks by each mistake.

She was only half finished when the recess bell rang. As students surged toward the door, she glanced up at Miss Brookner. The principal stood by her desk, his head near hers. Jean didn't want to interrupt their conversation.

Stacy skidded to a stop by her desk. "Coming?" she asked.

Jean laid her hand on the pile of ungraded papers. "I said I'd do these before lunchtime. I'm only half done. I guess I'm supposed to finish them before I go outside."

"I'm sure Miss Brookner doesn't expect you to miss recess."

"Maybe, but I can't ask her now." Jean watched her teacher leave with the principal. "I'd better stay in and finish. If I hurry, maybe I'll get done before recess is over."

"Suit yourself." Stacy hurried to catch up with the Nicholson twins.

Jean went back to correcting papers. She carefully checked one row of problems after another. The felt pen squeaked with every check mark.

A snicker from the back of the room surprised her. Turning around, she saw Jamison Andrews slouched over his desk in the corner. Jamison stayed in for more recesses than he went out, Jean thought. He messed around so much that he rarely had his work finished.

"How many brownie points do you get today?" he asked, sneering. "Or don't teacher's pets need brownie points?" His head fell toward his desk as he guffawed.

"Oh, shut up," Jean mumbled. "I'm working, if you want to know."

"I *know*, I *know*." He clasped his hand over his heart.

Determined to ignore him, Jean went back to grading papers. Five minutes later, Miss Brookner rushed back into the classroom.

"I'm surprised you're still here, Jean." She came to stand by her desk. "I had to take a phone call in the office. I left without thinking to tell you to go outside with the others."

Jean straightened the stack of math quizzes. "That's okay. I'm finished now." She handed the papers and pen to her teacher.

Walking back to the front of the room, her

teacher turned. "Jean, you should consider being a teacher one day. There's always a need for dependable people like you."

Jean smiled. It was worth it to have missed recess. Her teacher's good opinion mattered a lot to her.

While Miss Brookner finished some work at her desk, Jean leaned her head on her folded arms. There were only a few minutes of recess left, hardly enough time to go outside. She was mesmerized by the jerky second hand on the clock as she dreamed of a future day. . . .

She would again be grading papers, only this time after everyone else had gone home for the day. The heat in the building would be turned off, and her aching fingers stiff with cold as the hours wore on. But so great was her dedication that she barely noticed. One paper after another, she would give each assignment her total attention.

A deep voice would startle her. "And who might this hardworking young girl be?"

Jean would stare at the stranger in the doorway and pull her ragged woolen scarf tighter around her thin neck. Slowly, she'd recognize the head professor of the state teachers' college. His picture had been in recent teacher magazines. She couldn't imagine what he was doing in an elementary school in Goldridge.

He swept into the room, a cardboard tube clutched in his hand. "I knew I would find you here." He pulled at the reddish whiskers that hid his mouth.

"I have something for you—something extraordinary."

Wiping the ink smears from her trembling fingers, Jean gazed at the professor with awe. What could this famous man have for her?

Pulling a scroll of paper from the tube, he slowly unrolled it. "Your dedication to teaching, in spite of your age, has not gone unnoticed. I hereby grant you an honorary teaching degree from the state teachers' college." He handed the paper to her, bowing with a flourish. "You are the youngest person ever to receive an honorary teaching certificate."

Jean gasped, aware of the throbbing pulse in her neck. "But why me?"

The professor stroked his bushy beard. "We have been observing you carefully. Your talent and dedication are being wasted here. You should be instructing a class of eager young scholars of your own."

With tears brimming in her eyes, Jean humbly reached for the scroll. She was barely aware of the chilblains on her fingers. The letters on the scroll blurred as she read her name on the certificate. . . .

The bell clanged and Jean jumped, blinking and shaking her head as the other sixth-grade students filled the room. An honorary teacher no longer, she settled back into her chair for science class.

The rest of the day passed quickly for Jean. Between classes she peeked into her desk at the newspaper picture of the puppy. She was anxious to show the clipping to Stacy after school.

That afternoon as they walked home, Jean read the article aloud. "What do you think?" she asked at the end of the story. "Do you think my parents would let me get a puppy?"

"Maybe, if you paid for it yourself and promised to take care of it."

"Oh, I'd love taking care of a puppy! And I'm sure I could earn the fifteen dollars somehow."

"It can't hurt to ask. With summer vacation in eight weeks, you'd be home all the time to take care of it." Abruptly Stacy stopped, stamping her foot on the sidewalk. "Rats! I forgot my science book and we have that test tomorrow."

"What are you going to do?"

"Who knows? It's too late to go back to school. The room is probably locked already. Anyway I have to do my paper route now." She scuffed her tennis shoe on the sidewalk. "I don't suppose I could borrow your science book for a couple of hours? I'd return it before five o'clock. Then you could study for the test after supper."

Jean chewed her lower lip thoughtfully. "I guess so. I'm stopping at Grandma's on the way home. I planned to study after supper anyway."

"You're a life saver." Stacy tucked the science book under her arm. "It's terrific having a friend you can count on."

"You're sure you'll bring it back by supper time?"

"No problem." Stacy saluted as she turned the corner toward her home.

A block farther Jean turned south, the direction of her grandmother's house. She usually stopped there after school once a week.

Strolling up the sidewalk to the tiny white house, Jean felt herself relax instantly. It was always so calm and peaceful at her grandmother's. Orange and yellow tulips bloomed in pots on the porch railing. Window shades in the two front windows were pulled exactly halfway down. It always looked to Jean as if the house were falling asleep.

Jean knocked once and poked her head inside the front door. "Grandma? Are you home?"

"Is that you, Jeannie? Come on in. I'm in the kitchen." Her grandmother's voice was soft, yet reminded Jean of tinkling crystal.

Jean dropped her books in the living room on her way to the kitchen. In the small, bright kitchen, her grandmother sat hunched at a card table in the corner. Her ancient black typewriter rested on the table between stacks of papers. Her grandmother erased a page furiously, blew the erasure crumbs away and turned to smile.

"Have a seat at the table, Jeannie. Tell me about your day." She pulled the page from the typewriter. "I'll get us some rolls I baked just this afternoon. I could use a break." Jean's grandmother typed term papers for students at the local junior college.

"I'll get the milk, Grandma," Jean said hurriedly. It made her uncomfortable to have her grandmother wait on her. At home *she* was the one expected to jump up and get things. As she poured milk, she told her grandmother about the article on the Gold-ridge Animal Shelter.

"I remember seeing the picture last night," her grandmother said. "It's a worthy organization. And I agree with Stacy—it can't hurt to ask about it." She set a plate of warm cinnamon rolls on the table. "Now come sit down here and quit fussing at the sink."

Without thinking, Jean had run water in the dirty mixing bowl. "I can wash up these dishes for you, Grandma," she offered. "There aren't many."

Her grandmother waggled a finger at her. "Heavens, no. Just come sit down and talk to me. I don't get lots of visitors. I can do those dishes any-time."

Jean smiled sheepishly and sat down at the round oak table. She sometimes forgot that it was different at her grandmother's house.

For the next hour Jean told her grandmother about her day at school. She tried to make cor-recting math papers sound as exciting as possible. She didn't see how her day could interest a grownup, but Grandma seemed to enjoy hearing about it.

Jean knew her mother couldn't visit too often, since she worked full-time. Belinda was usually too busy with her social life. Mark spent most of his spare time with his friend Justin. Jean guessed her company, even though not very exciting, was better than nothing.

When the antique clock chimed five times, Jean gathered up her books to go home. Out on the front porch, her grandmother pulled her down for a hug.

"Take these rolls home to Belinda and Mark. Tell them to come over when they have time." She handed Jean a paper sack. "Good luck when you ask your parents about the puppy."

"Thanks, Grandma." Jean skipped down the steps, turned back and waved. "See you next week, if not before," she called, as she called every week.

Sauntering home, Jean decided to study for the science test a little while before supper. She hoped Stacy had returned her book. But when Jean got home, Belinda said Stacy hadn't come by. Shrugging, Jean went to change her clothes. She could always study after she ate.

After Belinda's supper, which included some funny-looking Chinese vegetables and a salad with alfalfa sprouts and fresh mushrooms, Jean hurriedly washed the dishes and stacked them. Still no Stacy. Jean waited by the living room window where she could see the television and watch the street at the same time.

By seven-thirty Jean was definitely worried. If Stacy didn't show up with her science book soon, she wouldn't have time to study for the test. By eight o'clock, Jean's worry had turned to anger. The more she brooded about it, the angrier she got.

Stacy *knew* she needed that book. Where was she?

Striding to the telephone, Jean punched the push-buttons. She fumed as a busy signal buzzed in her ear, then slammed down the receiver.

Stomping up the stairs to her room, Jean screamed inwardly at Stacy. She wished she had the nerve to say exactly what she felt. She'd love to tell Stacy what a skunk she was for taking advantage of her.

After viciously brushing her teeth, Jean sucked on her sore gums. Tossing her dirty clothes in the hamper, she pulled her flowered granny pajamas over her head. She was staring out the window when the telephone rang.

Running to the phone in her parents' bedroom, Jean stubbed her toe on the dresser. "Hello?" she gasped as she grabbed the receiver.

"Jean? Is that you?" The hoarse whisper could barely be heard.

Jean frowned. "Stacy?"

"Yes," she hissed. There was a long pause before she spoke again. "I can only talk for a minute. If my dad sees me, I'll have to hang up."

"What's going on?" Jean found herself whispering too.

"I left my bike in the driveway—again. My dad ran over it. It scratched up the car. He blew his stack! He grounded me, so I can't ask him to go over to your house."

"It's a little late anyway," Jean snapped. "When did this happen?"

"About six o'clock. I'm really sorry. I've been trying to get a chance to call you ever since."

Jean's anger flared. It had been more than two hours since the bike accident. Breathing hard, she slowly counted to ten.

"Jean, are you still there?"

Jean swallowed the angry words that rose inside her. "Listen. This is what I'll do. I'll pick you up early tomorrow morning. And I mean *early*. Then I can study before school starts." Jean knew her voice sounded hostile, but she didn't care.

Before she could say anything else, Stacy whispered a frantic, "Uh-oh. Bye." With a faint click, the line went dead.

Jean stared at the phone for a moment, then hung up. Back in her room, she climbed wearily into bed.

Clicking off her reading lamp, she flopped over on her back. Her resentment slowly drained away. It was replaced by real worry about her science test the next day.

Turning to face the wall, Jean pulled the quilt up to her chin. She'd set her alarm for six o'clock, hoping to get to Stacy's by seven. She knew she'd better try to get some sleep. It looked like tomorrow was going to be a long day.

3

Marshmallow

CLANK! SCREECH! CLUNK!

Jean turned over in bed and pulled the pillow over her head. Shutting her eyes firmly, she almost dozed off again.

"Bye, Joe! See you Friday!"

Groaning, Jean lifted her pillow and opened one eye. She glanced at the bedside clock in disgust.

5:56 a.m.

Sighing, Jean plumped up her pillow. At least she didn't have to get up yet. Yesterday had been hectic though. Out of breath, she'd arrived at Stacy's house at seven-fifteen. She'd studied her science book while Stacy ate breakfast. Jean feared she hadn't done too well on the test though.

Propping herself up on one elbow, Jean peered

through the yellow gingham curtains. From her upstairs bedroom she had a bird's-eye view of Joe Vitucci's garbage truck.

Joe climbed up into the cab. Leaning out the window, he waved to Mark standing on the curb. Jean shook her head as Mark scampered back to the house in his footed pajamas. Downstairs the front door slammed behind him.

Jean flopped back on her pillow, listening to Belinda's snores. She was tired of Mark waking her up twice a week at six o'clock. But Joe Vitucci was Mark's hero. Mark ran to meet him every time he came to pick up their garbage.

Jean wiggled her toes. Why couldn't Mark want to be something normal? Most little boys dreamed of being firemen or astronauts. But not Mark. His ambition was to be a garbage man like Joe. Only Mark called it being a "sanitation servant."

As the sun grew brighter behind the yellow curtains, Jean's mind wandered. She still hadn't asked her parents about getting a puppy. She hadn't found the right time yet. But she hoped to convince them soon, maybe over breakfast that morning.

With that goal in mind, Jean crawled out of bed and stretched. She tiptoed down the silent hall to the bathroom. She wanted to wash and dress before her parents woke up. If she hurried, she'd have time to put her plan into action.

It was still before seven when Jean glided silently down the carpeted stairs. In the kitchen Mark watched as she measured coffee into the coffee maker and started the bacon frying. Personally she hated the bitter smell of brewing coffee. But she'd noticed it usually put her father in a good mood to smell coffee and bacon when he walked into the kitchen.

Twenty minutes later her parents and a groggy Belinda shuffled into the kitchen. By that time the frozen orange juice was mixed and the eggs were fried. Jean's heart hammered under her ribs as she turned to hug her father.

"Morning, Dad," she said. "Coffee's ready." She hoped she sounded more nonchalant than she felt.

"Mmm-m-m-m." Her father sniffed the air like a bloodhound. "Sure smells good." He poured cups of coffee for himself and Jean's mother, then joined her at the table.

After Jean set the eggs and bacon on the table, she slid into her seat. Although her stomach flipflopped, she took an egg. Cutting it into tiny pieces, she pondered the best way to ask her parents about buying a puppy.

But when she glanced up, she caught the amused look that passed between her parents. Jean stared at her hands clasped in her lap. She felt her face begin to radiate heat. They suspected something was up, she just knew it.

"Do you want to ask us now, or later?" her father said. The laugh lines around his eyes crinkled.

Jean twisted her paper napkin into a knot. She hadn't fooled them one bit. Belinda could have protested her innocence, but Jean knew she was no good at acting. So she pulled the picture of the puppy from her jeans pocket. Unfolding it, she handed it to her father.

"This article and picture were in the newspaper last Friday night. The Goldridge Animal Shelter is overcrowded. They're looking for good homes for the cats and dogs they have." She took a deep breath. "I was wondering if maybe I could save my money and adopt a puppy," she ended in a rush.

Jean noticed her fingers were shaking. She laced them tightly together. The only sounds she heard were Belinda's yawns and the gentle whir of the refrigerator. Quietly her mother and father read the article.

"What do you think, Dan?" her mother asked, getting up to pour more coffee.

Jean's father winked at her. "I'm sure Jean would take good care of a puppy," he said. He scratched his overnight growth of beard. "But you need fifteen dollars. Where would you get that much money?"

"I have a couple ideas." Jean held up two fingers. "First, I could save my dollar allowance each week. Also, I could carry a Thermos with my lunch. That way I'd save the two dollars you give me every week for milk and soup at school. In five weeks I could have the fifteen dollars." She chewed her lower lip as her father drummed his fingers on the table.

Belinda seemed to awake from a trance. Blinking furiously, she gaped at her father. "A dog? Jean's going to get a dog?" She sounded like Jean was intending to buy a pet alligator. "I want to state right now that I oppose any such idea! Dogs carry fleas. Fleas can hop all over and get on people! And I won't have dog hair all over our bedroom. And you know how dogs smell—"

"Okay, we get your point," her father said. "But if anyone gets a puppy, the animal will stay outside."

"I'm afraid that brings up a few other expenses," her mother said slowly. "The puppy will need a license, a doghouse, a dish or two, and also a leash and collar. Those things cost money. I'm sure we can afford to buy the dog food, but you will have to provide the other things, Jean."

Jean's good spirits wilted for a minute at the thought of the extra money she'd need. But even if it took a little longer, she still wanted a puppy. Now more than ever. "Does that mean you'll let me save for a puppy then? That is, if I can earn the money for everything?"

Her father swallowed his egg before answering. "You've always been dependable and responsible. If you want to save for a puppy, go ahead."

Belinda groaned. She shook her tousled curls and dropped her head on her folded arms.

Mark whistled shrilly, jumped up and down, and spilled his orange juice. "I bet you won't have to buy a leash or dog dishes or anything, Jean." He grinned as if he knew a huge secret. "Joe says people throw away the neatest junk in their garbage. I'll ask him to look for dog stuff for you."

Jean nearly choked on a piece of bacon. "You want Joe to hunt through his garbage for me?" She tried not to laugh. Mark appeared very serious.

Belinda rolled her eyes and clutched her stomach. "I'm going to be sick," she muttered.

Mark nodded eagerly. "It would save you a lot of money."

"That's okay, Mark. Thanks anyway." Jean poured Mark some more juice. "I can earn enough money to buy what my puppy will need." *My puppy.* Jean smiled. She loved the sound of those words.

After hugging her parents, Jean slathered peanut butter on some bread for a sandwich to pack for lunch. She winced as she remembered what she had intended to buy at school. That day they were having her favorite lunch—spaghetti. Her mouth watered at the thought. Then she remembered that a puppy was waiting for her at the Goldridge Animal Shelter. Eating peanut butter sandwiches seemed a small price to pay.

After getting permission to visit the animal shelter after school, Jean pedaled off to school on her bike.

The day dragged by. Jean had a hard time concentrating. She couldn't wait to find the puppy she would someday take home. She had no idea what breed of puppy she wanted. But deep down, Jean knew there was a special puppy at the shelter, waiting just for her.

After school Jean raced to the schoolyard, strapped down her books and jumped on her bike. Pedaling out Main Street, she spotted the animal shelter sign. She skidded to a stop in front of a shedlike building and leaned on her handle bars. Jean frowned. It seemed too quiet. She had expected to see barking dogs in pens and hear mewing noises drifting out from the windows.

Jean took three deep gulps of air. Then she pushed open a door with a sign that read "Come in—we're open." She entered a waiting room with a counter at the back. A door behind the counter stood open. The meowing and barking she had expected came from that direction.

Jean moved around the empty room, studying posters about vaccinations. After waiting for ten minutes, she spotted a bell on the counter. "Ring for Service" said the faded sign taped by the bell. Timidly, she touched the bell. The piercing *ding!* made her jump.

"Coming!" a friendly voice called from somewhere beyond the door.

Within a minute a tall, lanky man hurried into the waiting room. He rubbed his totally bald head with a large hand. "Can I help you with something?" he asked. A grin split his face from ear to ear—much like someone cracking an egg, Jean thought.

"My name is Jean Harvey. I read your story in the

newspaper." Studying the man's homey face, Jean relaxed. "I want to buy a puppy as soon as I have enough money."

The gangly man wiped his hand on his trousers and held it out. Jean's fingers were swallowed up in his huge hand. "My name's Mr. Sorensen. I'm in charge here at the Goldridge Animal Shelter. You caught me in the middle of feeding the cats." He motioned for her to follow him through the open door. "We can talk while I finish. Then I'll show you the puppies."

Jean nodded and followed him into the next room. Wire cages were stacked three deep around the room. All sorts of cats peered through the wires. Their colors ranged from pure black to yellow to striped. Most of the cats looked full grown. Two cages also held litters of kittens.

Mr. Sorensen moved quickly from one cage to the next. He fed each older cat a cupful of dry cat food from a large bag. Then, after putting clean shredded newspaper on the bottom of each cage, he moved to the next one.

He chatted with Jean as he worked, glancing at his watch every few minutes. Jean wondered why he was in such a rush. She followed him from cage to cage, stopping to admire a family of tiger kittens that nestled close to their mother.

"All done." Mr. Sorensen folded down the top of the cat food bag. "If you'll follow me, now I can show you our dogs. Thanks for being patient while I finished the feedings. We're a little shorthanded right now." He chuckled softly. "Actually we're always shorthanded. The animal shelter budget doesn't allow for many assistants."

He led the way down a long white hallway. They passed an office on one side. Glancing in the open door, Jean noticed a cage on the floor. Inside, a large black dog slept.

Jean pointed to the dozing animal. "Is that dog waiting for its owner?"

"I'm afraid that that dog is sick. I'm waiting for the vet to come and check him over." He continued down the hallway and opened the door at the end.

Deep barking and shrill yipping filled the room. Jean had never seen so many shapes and sizes of dogs. Each dog's pen reminded her of a cage at the zoo. Half of each cage was inside, half outside. The dogs could go through small hinged doors at the back and spend time in the cage outside.

As in the cat room, most of the dog cages were filled with grown animals. Walking down the cement aisle between the cages, Jean studied each of the dogs. She knew she wanted a puppy, but she didn't want to ignore all the bigger dogs. She felt she would hurt their feelings if she walked by their cages without even a glance.

Mr. Sorensen explained the good points of every dog they passed. He also informed her that the fifteen dollar fee would be applied towards shots for her pet. Jean made a mental note. Shots were another thing she had overlooked in counting her expenses.

After passing a dozen cages, three which held puppies, Jean grew uneasy. Maybe the puppy she had in mind wasn't there after all. She wasn't exactly sure what she wanted, she admitted to herself. But she knew she hadn't yet seen *her* dog.

At the second to the last cage, Jean sucked in her breath sharply. In the cage was a mother cocker spaniel surrounded by puppies.

"These were born six weeks ago," Mr. Sorensen said. "It's hard to find a friendlier dog than a cocker spaniel."

The puppies were mostly spotted, black and brown and white. One puppy was solid black. Mr. Sorensen said he already had an adopter.

But Jean wasn't observing the black puppy. She wasn't drawn to any of the puppies that tumbled over each other and climbed on the mother dog. The puppy Jean wanted was in the back corner of the cage. She was light tan all over with the biggest brown eyes Jean had ever seen.

The puppy lay quietly, studying Jean. Her droopy ears brushed the floor. Her plump sides breathed in and out. While the other puppies barked and romped and wrestled on top of the mother dog, she quietly behaved herself. In return for her good behavior, she was ignored. Jean knew just how the puppy felt.

Jean stuck her fingers through the cage and wiggled them. "Come here. Come a little closer." She smiled at the puppy's plump tan body. "You look like a big toasted marshmallow," she said, chuckling.

"That little cocker interest you?" Mr. Sorensen asked. "I should warn you that she's pretty quiet. One of the other puppies might be more fun to play with."

Worried, Jean glanced up at the tall man. "She's healthy, isn't she?"

"Oh, yes, she's in perfect health. You could count on her to be a nice quiet dog. She's just not as frisky as the others."

Jean straightened and looked Mr. Sorensen in the eye. "Just because she's quiet and doesn't cause trouble doesn't mean she won't be a terrific pet." She spoke firmly. "At my house she won't have to compete with other puppies. Then she might be more lively and playful."

Mr. Sorensen scratched his pink scalp with a long finger. "You may be right about that. If you're sure this is the puppy you want, I'll get her out now." He reached for the latch on the door.

"I'd love to hold her a minute, but I can't take her home today. I don't have all the money saved yet." She pulled four crumpled dollar bills from her pocket. "But I can make a deposit on her. Then I could pay you three dollars a week—maybe more if

I get some odd jobs. In a few weeks I'll have her all paid for." Jean chewed her lower lip as she waited for Mr. Sorensen's answer.

"I'm afraid we don't take deposits. The animals have to be paid for the day they're taken home." At Jean's worried expression, he quickly added, "No one else is interested in this puppy yet. If someone asks about her before you've saved enough money, I'll let you know." He pulled a card and pencil stub from his pocket. "Write down your name and phone number. I'll put the card in my office. Do you have a name for your dog?"

Jean studied the puppy, then nodded. "Marshmallow. Because she looks like a toasted marshmallow."

Mr. Sorensen laughed. "Good choice." He added the puppy's name to the card.

A shrill *ding-ding!* sounded from the waiting room.

"Better see who it is," Mr. Sorensen said, quickly unlocking the cage door for Jean. "Come up to the waiting room when you're finished." Glancing at his watch, he trotted past the dog cages and disappeared through the door.

Jean stepped into the cage and pulled the door closed behind her. While the puppies frolicked around her feet, she inched over to the corner of the cage. Stooping, she gently picked up the plump puppy. Holding her close, Jean stroked the soft fur on her back.

In less than a minute Mr. Sorensen returned with a young mother and three children. Jean overheard the mother saying they lived on a farm and wanted a large dog. He had to be "friendly with children, but also bark loudly at strangers." When Jean was satisfied that the woman couldn't possibly want Marshmallow, she turned to leave. She set the cocker spaniel down in the corner again. The tan puppy cocked her head to one side, as if asking a question.

"I'll be back, Marshmallow," Jean whispered. "I promise."

Wandering back down the long hall, Jean paused in the doorway of Mr. Sorensen's office. The sick dog in the cage looked up and whimpered.

Jean glanced down the empty hallway. She could hear Mr. Sorensen still talking with the lady and three children. No one else appeared to be in the building. She decided it surely wouldn't hurt to try to comfort the sick animal.

"Hi, there," Jean crooned, stepping nearer the cage. The long-haired black dog raised his head slowly. "Are you sick? Can I get you something?"

Jean studied the lock on the cage. She wished she could open the little door and pet the dog. She poked her fingers through the wire to stroke him, but the holes were too small. She could barely touch his head.

"Get back!" a voice bellowed behind her. "Get your fingers out of that cage!"

Jerking her hand back, Jean swung around at the

angry voice. In the doorway stood a young man. His black eyes blazed. His faded blue jeans and plaid shirt fit him loosely. He gripped a small black bag in his right hand.

Stepping back quickly, Jean stammered, "I'm—I'm sorry. The dog seemed lonesome and Mr. Sorensen was busy. I know I shouldn't be in here, but I thought—"

"I don't care what you thought." The man's thick eyebrows drew together. "I came to check this dog—for rabies. You could have been bitten, sticking your fingers in there like that."

Jean opened her eyes wide. "I thought rabid animals foamed at the mouth and acted crazy." She edged toward the door, anxious to get away from the angry veterinarian. As she reached the exit, Mr. Sorensen appeared in the doorway and blocked her escape.

"Hi, Brent! I didn't know you'd arrived." He stepped into his office. "Have you had a chance to examine the dog?"

"Not yet." The vet glanced at Jean.

Jean barely breathed. Was he going to tell Mr. Sorensen where he had found her? She stared at the floor.

But he seemed to have forgotten she was there. "What makes you think he may have rabies?" he asked Mr. Sorensen.

"Well, he's usually such a frisky dog." The animal shelter manager spread his huge hands wide. "But the last two or three days he's been sleeping a lot. Not interested in food or anything. Reminded me of that dog we saw last year that had rabies."

Jean knew she could leave without anyone noticing, but she was too interested in their conversation.

The vet nodded. "I remember. Had us fooled at first." He bent down to study the dog closer. "He doesn't seem to be salivating much, though."

Without thinking, Jean spoke up. "What does that mean?"

The vet turned and frowned at her. "Why do you want to know?"

Jean blinked at his unfriendliness. "I'm just interested. I'm going to adopt a dog soon."

Snapping open his bag, he said, "Rabies is a virus that attacks the central nervous system. Man is infected by saliva in the bite of a rabid animal." He stood up slowly, pulling on some gloves. "An animal with rabies *can* show violent behavior. Or he may be unusually sleepy with an excessive flow of saliva. The dog may even lose his bark. Soon the animal is paralyzed."

Jean shuddered. She hated to imagine that sad-looking dog paralyzed. And she knew that rabid animals had to be killed.

Dismissing Jean, the vet turned to Mr. Sorensen. "He's probably not rabid. There's no extra saliva that I can see. But we'd better observe him for another week and see."

Jean backed into the hallway as Brent reached

into his black bag. Suddenly she felt in the way. Turning at the sound of footsteps, she saw Mr. Sorensen right behind her.

"That Brent Davis, he's a fine vet. I always call him." He walked beside Jean, taking long easy strides. "You can always count on him to come right away and know what's wrong."

"I hope the dog is all right," Jean said. Remembering Marshmallow, she asked, "Is it all right if I visit my puppy sometimes?"

"Anytime you like."

They passed through the room of cats and out to the waiting area. "Thanks for showing me your animals, Mr. Sorensen. See you next week." Jean waved as she went out the front door.

Pedaling home, Jean's thoughts drifted from Mr. Sorensen to Marshmallow to the sick dog. The sick dog made her think of Brent Davis.

According to Mr. Sorensen, Brent Davis was dependable. Mr. Sorensen said you could always count on him. But Jean doubted if Brent Davis worried about what others thought of him.

Reluctantly she smiled. One thing was sure. Remembering the way the vet had barked at her—for her own good, Jean admitted—she bet that *nobody* walked all over *him*!

4

Favor for a Friend

During Friday afternoon's art class, Mrs. Kemper said the class could make anything they wanted out of papier-mâché. Jean decided to mold a figure of Marshmallow. She would take it home the next week and put it in her room. The statue would remind her why she ate peanut butter sandwiches every day and hadn't bought a candy bar in two weeks.

With ten minutes to spare, Jean slapped on the last gooey strip of paper. After washing her hands and desk, the dismissal bell rang.

Grabbing her books, Jean joined Stacy who was elbow deep in papier-mâché. Stacy scraped sticky goo from her hands and picked strips of newspaper from her arms and legs.

"I have a big favor to ask you," Stacy said. "I'm

supposed to deliver my newspapers by four o'clock. If I don't, I'm in big trouble with my customers. But it's going to take me forever to clean up this mess."

"Do you want some help cleaning up?"

"Well, I had something else in mind." She bent to peel off strips of newspaper that were glued to the floor around her. "I'd like to stay and finish this pot of tulips. I'm making these flowers for my mom's birthday." She held up a wad of soggy newspaper stuck on the end of a stick. "I wondered if you'd deliver my papers—just this once."

"You're kidding! I can't do your paper route." Jean shook her head firmly and backed away.

Stacy held up ten sticky, pleading fingers. "It really isn't hard. You could use my bike with the basket on the front. It's outside in the bike rack."

"But I've never been on your route. How would I know where to deliver the papers?" Jean backed up a few more steps.

"That's easy! I'll write down the addresses. The twenty-two houses are all in a five-block area. You just pick up the bundle of newspapers on the corner of Seventh and Jefferson and deliver them." Stacy smiled hopefully. "Please?"

Jean felt trapped. There was really no reason not to do this favor for Stacy. Since it was Friday, she didn't need to hurry home and do her homework. Half angry at herself, she felt her resolve begin to melt.

Her shoulders sagged. "How long does it take to deliver papers to twenty-two houses?"

"About half an hour, maybe a little more." Stacy scribbled a list of addresses on a piece of notebook paper. "Just go in the order I've listed. You'll be done in no time."

Sourly, Jean took the list of addresses and shuffled up the aisle. Jamison Andrews, always the tormentor, stuck out his foot and nearly tripped her. He seemed to sense just the right time to be most annoying. Good old Jamison!

"Get your foot back," Jean growled. "I'm in a hurry."

Rushing to the bike rack in front of the building, she felt her face begin to burn. What was the matter with her anyway? Couldn't she ever say "no"?

Dumping her books into the basket, Jean pedaled down the street toward Seventh and Jefferson. As she rounded the corner, she spotted the bundle of newspapers on the grass near the street.

Braking, she coasted down the block. She stopped at the corner and reached for the newspapers. After inspecting the bundle, Jean gritted her teeth. Stacy had failed to mention that the papers were tied together with heavy twine.

Working at the knot, Jean wondered how her friend got the papers loose. Stacy must use a knife or something, she decided. Jean tried to chew through the twine. As the cord cut into her fingers, she heard thunder rumbling softly in the distance.

She tugged the knot back and forth, finally sliding it over to the corner and off. She piled the loose papers on top of her three books in the shallow bike basket. Jean had to hold one hand on the blowing papers as she pedaled down the street.

Reviewing her list of addresses, Jean turned at Elm Street. Rolls of thunder grew louder and closer together. She glanced uneasily at the gray clouds billowing up in the west.

At the first house on her list Jean carefully folded the newspaper in thirds. When she tossed it the paper landed squarely in the middle of the porch. Nodding with satisfaction, Jean continued down the street. Stacy was right. This was going to be easy.

As each paper landed near its target, Jean's confidence grew. She began throwing them from farther away. At the seventh house she barely coasted to a stop before hurling the paper. It disappeared in shaggy bushes near the front door.

Sighing, Jean dismounted to go retrieve it.

Down on her hands and knees, she searched in the bushes. Her bare arms were soon scratched and itchy. When she located the paper, she pulled it out and flung it toward the front step.

Sitting back on her heels, Jean felt two drops of rain hit her arm. She muttered under her breath as she scanned the darkening sky. The blackest clouds still appeared to be far away. She decided to hurry anyway.

Jean checked her watch as she reached the next

house. She raised her arm to throw the paper. Without warning a snarling dog shot around the corner of the porch. It lunged toward her, its lips curled back over sharp yellowed teeth.

Jean screamed and jumped back on the bike. Glancing over her shoulder, she saw the savage dog struggling at the end of a heavy chain. With tremendous relief Jean realized it couldn't get any closer.

Her heart thudding, Jean folded the paper and pitched it near the front door. She kept a wary eye on the growling dog as she pedaled off.

As she turned the corner at the third block, the black sky opened up. Light sprinkles abruptly changed to a steady rain. Before she could pull under a tree for protection, Jean's shirt was soaked. Her brown bangs were plastered to her forehead. She saw with dismay that her newspapers on top were also wet.

Shivering, Jean huddled under the tree for almost fifteen minutes. By that time the downpour had turned into a light drizzle. She felt it was safe to finish the route.

Jean folded several papers into thirds and started down the block. At the last house on Elm Street an old woman stood hunched over under an ancient black umbrella. Her piercing eyes and fierce scowl reminded Jean of the wicked witch in *The Wizard of Oz*.

She parked Stacy's bike and walked up the sidewalk to the old lady. She opened her mouth to apologize for the soggy paper. "I'm sorry about—"

"You're late." The woman snatched the paper. Peering closer at Jean, she snapped, "Who are you, anyway?"

"I'm Jean Harvey, a friend of your regular delivery girl. I was caught in the rain—"

"Whoever you are, the paper should have been here thirty-five minutes ago. I always read it right after I feed my cat. My paper wasn't inside the screen door where it should have been." She glared down her long pointed nose at Jean.

"I've never delivered papers before. I'm sorry that—"

"This paper is all wet! How do you expect me to read this paper? The pages are all stuck together!" She tapped the newspaper with a gnarled finger. "I pay good money for dry newspapers delivered on time."

"Let me trade you for a drier paper then. I have some—"

The old woman jerked back her wet paper. "Oh, no, you don't! I won't let you destroy this evidence. I'm going to call your boss and have you fired!"

"But I'm just a substitute. Your regular girl will be—"

"I have no more to say to the likes of you," the woman snapped. She turned and hobbled into her house. She peered at Jean through gauzy curtains at her front window.

Shaking with anger, Jean ran back to the bike. She jumped on and pedaled as fast as she could to the next block.

The nerve of that old witch, Jean thought. *Who does she think she is anyway? She wouldn't even let me explain why I was late.*

Jean's fuming was interrupted as her legs abruptly jerked to a stop. She coasted down the sidewalk, but couldn't pedal. Looking down, Jean saw her right pants leg was caught in the bike chain.

Jean hopped along on her free leg until she stopped the bike. She balanced herself carefully and yanked at her pants leg. After several hard jerks, it came loose. Her jeans were smeared with black grease. Teeth marks from the chain bit into the denim.

Jean was relieved to have her leg free until she saw the chain. It had come off when she jerked her pants loose. It hung from the bike in a limp loop.

Jean laid the bike on its side and tried to replace the chain. The greasy links slipped in her fingers. She couldn't stretch it enough to fit over the sprockets. After ten minutes she gave up and wiped her greasy hands on the wet grass.

She shivered as a breeze blew against her wet clothes and hair. Studying her list, she counted the remaining addresses. Seven people still waited for their newspapers.

Jean could think of no choice except to walk the bike the rest of the way. Slowly she made her way down the street, finishing Stacy's route. By the time she arrived home, she was sneezing and shaking all over.

Later that evening Jean sat swaddled in an old bathrobe in her bedroom, her feet soaking in hot Epsom salts water. She took turns sneezing and blowing her nose. Resentment of her best friend grew. All because of Stacy, Jean thought, she'd probably caught pneumonia and ruined her best pair of jeans.

Her anger at Stacy slowly faded and was replaced with irritation at herself. She hadn't wanted to do the paper route in the first place. So why had she?

Jean shifted uncomfortably in the chair. Was she afraid to say *no*? Would people like her if she stopped doing all the things they expected of her? Would her friends and family need her if she changed?

Frankly, Jean admitted to herself, she was afraid to find out.

5

Footprints Up My Back

Jean sneezed violently as she followed her mother and Belinda through the double doors of the shopping center. Usually she liked shopping trips, but today she ached all over. The Saturday morning crowd jostled her as she stopped to blow her nose.

Jean rarely bought new clothes, but she'd had another growth spurt lately. Her pants and skirts were two inches too short. Jean headed for the racks in the junior department. Finding her size, she thumbed expertly through the rainbow colors. She wanted to buy her new slacks quickly and go home.

"Do I have to get blue pants again, Mom?" Jean asked. Blue was the one color that coordinated with her two best shirts and her sweater.

Her mother looked over Jean's shoulder. "Not

if you prefer another color. But the pattern can't be too wild and the pants need to have a large hem. I'm sure we'll have to let them down later."

Jean showed her a tan pair of slacks with dark brown stitching. In her other hand she held up a white pair of slacks with a fancy design on the back pockets. Jean thought the white pants looked terrific, especially for spring and summer.

Belinda poked her head around the end of the rack. "Come here a minute, Mom! I found the prettiest pair of—" She stopped abruptly and gawked at the slacks Jean held. "You're not getting *another* dull pair of pants, are you? Get something colorful for a change!"

Jean turned her back on Belinda. "What do you think, Mom? I really like the white pants best. Both pairs are in my size and cost the same."

A slight frown creased her mother's forehead. "The white pants are pretty. But I'm not sure how practical they are. White clothes show dirt terribly."

Jean had known her mother would say that. "I guess the tan ones are all right anyway." She returned the white pants to the rack.

"I think that's very sensible, dear," her mother said, nodding with approval.

Draping the tan pants over her arm, Jean turned toward the checkout counters. "Can we go home now?" she asked. Her head pounded over each temple. "I don't feel too good."

Belinda blocked her path, her feet planted wide apart. "Not yet, we aren't. There's something I want to show Mom in my size." She clutched her mother's arm and pulled her down the aisle.

Straggling behind, Jean wondered what Belinda had discovered this time. More alligator key rings or satin bedroom slippers? Or maybe another fake fur vest with brass buttons.

Jean rounded the corner and saw Belinda holding a pair of bright pink jeans in front of her. "Aren't these just perfect?" she squealed. "Rob will just love them!"

Her mother shook her head and laughed. "But Rob isn't paying for them. And neither am I."

"I'll pay for them with my babysitting money." Belinda patted her bulging purse. "They match my new fuzzy pink sweater perfectly."

"But aren't you forgetting something?" her mother asked. "It's only a few weeks until the MORP. You may need a few things for the dance. Maybe you should save your money."

"But I just *have* to have these pink jeans. I'll *die* if I don't get them!"

Jean rolled her eyes toward the ceiling. She doubted very much if Belinda would drop dead right there in the store if she didn't get the jeans.

Her mother shrugged. "It's your money, I guess. But don't come to me for money later. You may end up wearing these jeans to your MORP dance."

Jean could just picture that. The MORP was the ninth-graders' dressy spring dance at the Y. It was held the same night as the high school prom. MORP was "prom" spelled backwards and Jean thought it was a dumb name. It was a girl-ask-boy dance. Of course Belinda was taking Rob.

Belinda twirled around with the jeans in front of her. "I can't wait to wear these. Rob's eyes will pop out when he sees them on me. They practically glow in the dark."

Her mother laughed. "They're colorful, all right. But not very practical."

Belinda pouted prettily. "I know I'm not as sensible as Jean about clothes. That's just the way I am. There's enough time to be sensible when I'm old." She snapped her fingers. "Simply think of me as a peacock. You know, flashy and flamboyant. Jean's more like a little brown wren."

"I never thought of it that way." Her mother chuckled as she led the way to the cash register.

Following behind with her tan slacks, Jean frowned with resentment. Her mother had praised her for being sensible and practical. But somehow Jean was left with the feeling that she was drab and colorless. Still sneezing, she decided maybe she was.

At home, Jean had trouble swallowing her lunch, but even with her sore throat, she finished before her sister. Belinda was practicing "behavior modification" to make her meal last longer. She chewed every morsel of food thirty times. Between bites she dropped her fork with a clank and sipped her water.

"If you would slow your eating down, you wouldn't consume nearly so many calories," she lectured her mother between mouthfuls. "It's better for your digestion too." She cut another tiny bite of tuna.

"If I took as long to eat as you do, my soup would get cold," her mother replied. "Anyway, today I'm in a hurry. I promised to put up Grandma's window screens right after lunch. We've had some warm days lately. She'd like to be able to open her windows."

"Can I glo und blay with Thustin?" Mark's words were garbled by the raspberry sour ball he popped into his mouth for dessert.

"No, you can't go and play with Justin." Mrs. Harvey pushed back her chair. "You stay here. Belinda will keep an eye on you until I get home. If Dad gets off work early, you can go play."

Jean put her plate in the sink. "I think I'll crawl into bed with a book while you're gone. Tell Grandma I'll see her next week."

"I will. Take care of that cold." She waved and closed the door behind her.

Taking a cup of hot chocolate with her, Jean trudged up the stairs to her bedroom. The blaring from the TV lessened when she shut her door. In half an hour she had finished her hot chocolate and her last mystery. She closed the book with a sigh. Jean loved whodunits.

Down the hall the telephone jangled, stopping after only one ring. Jean listened to see if Belinda yelled upstairs. When she didn't hear anything, she presumed the call was for her sister.

Jean scrunched down under her quilt. Maybe she'd take a nap. And yet she hated to face the rest of the weekend without a book. She pushed back her covers and crawled out of bed.

Pulling on a sweater, she grabbed her three library books to return. Maybe the short walk uptown would pep her up, she thought. She might even run into Stacy at the library.

Opening the door, Jean was nearly knocked down as Belinda rushed into their bedroom.

"Whoops! Sorry." Belinda raced past her and jerked open a dresser drawer. "That was Rob on the phone. We're going to Scalla's for an ice cream cone. I want to wear my new pink jeans."

Jean clutched her books. "Is Mom home already?"

"No, she's not." Belinda's muffled voice drifted from the closet. "But I knew you were reading and wouldn't mind watching Mark for a while."

"But I was just leaving," Jean protested.

Belinda continued as if she hadn't heard her. "I should be back in half an hour." She emerged from the walk-in closet in her pink jeans and a fluffy pink sweater. Patting her curls, she waltzed out the door.

"Hey, wait a minute!" Jean trotted after her.

Downstairs the doorbell rang. Jumping down the

last three steps, Belinda dashed to the front door. Jean could hear Rob's voice mumble something, then Belinda's answering laugh.

As Jean reached the front door, Belinda was pulling it closed behind her. Yanking it open again, Jean shouted, "I'm *not* going to stay and watch Mark. It's your job! I'm going uptown! Right now!"

Belinda ignored her shouts and linked her arm through Rob's. Jean slammed the door. She dropped her books with a clatter and headed to the living room.

There, Mark stared as if hypnotized at a science fiction movie. At least Jean thought it was science fiction. Purple plants were eating people who bobbed up and down in what looked like split pea soup.

Jean caught her reflection in the mirror over the fireplace. Her green-flecked eyes snapped. Her clenched teeth made her jaw look square.

"She's not going to do this to me again," she muttered. "I just won't let her." She turned and called to Mark.

"What dlid you slay?"

"I said I'm going to the library. I should be home in half an hour. If Mom gets home before that, tell her Belinda went to get an ice cream cone with Rob." Jean didn't know if Mark was listening or not. Shrugging, she grabbed her books and stalked out the front door.

Jean marched down the sidewalk. With each step,

waves of guilt washed over her. But she was determined to fight it.

I won't go back and cover for Belinda again, she told herself sternly. *I have rights too. I'm through getting walked on.*

Soon she had covered a full block. She knew she was right. But she kept remembering that Mark was only six years old.

Part of her argued that Mark could take care of himself for a little while. What could happen to him while he watched TV? If he somehow hurt himself, no one could blame *her* for it. Babysitting him was Belinda's job. *She* would get the blame.

At the end of the second block, Jean's footsteps were dragging. Terrifying pictures flashed through her mind. A kidnapper breaking into the house . . . A fire trapping Mark in flames . . . Mark being electrocuted by a short in the TV . . .

Sighing deeply, Jean turned around.

Back home, she checked on Mark. He was still watching monster plants gobble people. Picking up a magazine, she went to the kitchen. She grabbed two bananas and collapsed at the table.

By the time she finished her second banana, Jean's anger had cooled. The decorator magazine was boring, so she decided to join Mark in watching man-eating plants destroy the world.

Lying on the couch, Jean found herself wishing she had a sister-eating plant for Belinda. She would keep it in a big pot in their bedroom and feed it plenty of fertilizer. Then when Belinda pulled another stunt . . .

"*Grullug.*"

Jean glanced up. "What did you say? It's hard to understand you with that candy in your mouth."

Mark pointed to his throat. *"Hhrullgh—"*

"Mark?" Jean rolled off the couch. "Are you all right?" She ran to him and dropped to the floor.

Clutching his throat, Mark croaked out a hoarse sound. His eyes protruded as he gasped for breath. In horror, Jean watched his face turn a ghastly purple. Mark was choking!

"Hhrullgh! Hhrulgh!"

Jean quickly darted behind her little brother. Mark thrashed in her arms as she applied the sharp hug below the ribs she'd learned in the Y's first-aid class. Once, then again—hard. A green sour ball popped out of Mark's mouth and rolled a few inches across the carpet.

Mark collapsed onto the floor, gulping air. Soon his face turned its usual healthy pink. Smiling feebly, he asked, "Where's my sour ball?"

"Are you all right?" Jean sat back, weak with relief. "You really scared me!"

Mark stretched his arms over his head. "I'm okay, except it feels like you broke my ribs. Did you have to hug me so hard?" He rolled over to watch the rest of his TV program.

Jean trembled as she picked up the fuzzy sour ball. Taking the candy to the kitchen to throw away, she found her knees were like jelly. They wobbled crazily.

A question played in her mind like a broken record. *What if I hadn't come back? What if I hadn't come back?*

Sinking into a chair at the kitchen table, Jean pushed her damp bangs back off her forehead. She hated to admit, even to herself, how scared she had been. She'd thought Mark was going to choke to death right in front of her.

As she stared out the window, Jean pictured a day in the near future. . . .

She would come home from Stacy's house late in the afternoon. Opening the front door, she'd be engulfed by swirling black smoke.

Coughing and choking, she'd blindly fight her way to the living room. There a blaze burned out of control, spreading across the room from the smoky fireplace. Mark lay face down on the rug in a crumpled heap!

Her eyes smarting, Jean peered through the smoke. Where was Belinda? She was supposed to be watching Mark!

Tears streamed down Jean's blistered face. Her trembling knees almost buckled as she hoisted her limp brother over her shoulder. She struggled bravely under his weight as she stumbled out the front door. Jean gulped fresh cool air into her burning lungs.

Dropping to her knees, she gratefully placed Mark on the soot-covered grass. The last thing she remembered before fainting gracefully was the sound of distant sirens . . . darkness, and then . . . a stark hospital room. She gazed lovingly at the anxious faces of her parents and brother as they hovered over her oxygen tent.

On the other side of her bed Belinda cried softly into a hospital washcloth, her scorched clothing in shreds, her dainty arms streaked with black soot. Her sister had entered the burning house to rescue her new pink jeans! She clutched the torn, grimy pants in her shaking hands.

In spite of the excruciating pain, Jean smiled wanly at her formerly beautiful sister. Belinda's perfect strawberry-blonde curls had been burned off. Only short spikey hairs stuck out from her scorched scalp. . . .

Slam! The front door snapped Jean out of her daydream. She heard Belinda humming a popular tune in the hallway. Pushing back her chair, Jean walked slowly through the house.

Belinda and Rob stood inside the front door, holding hands. They were nearly the same height, but Belinda always slouched when Rob was there. That way she could look up into Rob's dark eyes and flutter her own dark lashes. Jean thought the goofy expressions they made at each other were revolting. Without a word she picked up her library books and walked around them.

Belinda called after her. "Thanks for watching Mark. I'll take over now."

Jean twisted the doorknob, then turned back to her sister. Anger bubbled just under the surface. "It's about time—"

"Oh, by the way," Belinda interrupted, "I saw this pair of barrettes in Callison's window on the way home. I thought you might like them. Sort of a 'get well' present." She handed Jean two curved barrettes, a rainbow painted on each one.

Jean stared at the colorful barrettes as she slowly let out her breath. How could she say anything now? Was this Belinda's way of saying she was sorry she'd run out on her? Jean pushed the angry words down and produced a half-hearted smile.

"Thanks. I'll wear them tomorrow." Avoiding their eyes, Jean pulled the door closed behind her.

On the way to the library Jean met her mother coming home from her grandmother's. Jean decided not to say anything about Belinda. It was over— Mark was all right—and her mom would only be upset.

At the library Jean chose three books by her favorite mystery writer. On the way home she decided to stop at Grandma's herself. Seated in the kitchen, Jean told her about Mark choking on the sour ball and Belinda running out on her again.

". . . and I'm tired of *always* having to change my plans to fit Belinda's," Jean said, finishing her angry outburst.

Jean's grandmother turned from cleaning her typewriter keys. "I would have gladly watched Mark for you. You only had to call me."

"But Mom and Dad expect me to take over for Belinda."

"Maybe, but I'm not sure you're thinking about this clearly." Grandma covered her typewriter. "Of course there's nothing wrong with your being dependable. It's very important." She paused and took a deep breath.

"But?"

"But being dependable isn't the same as being walked on. No one deserves that kind of treatment."

Jean opened her eyes wide. She'd never thought about it exactly that way before. Could she be dependable without everyone taking advantage of her?

On the way home, Jean thought about her grandmother's words. She didn't know if there was anything she could do to change Belinda, but one thing was sure. She certainly felt walked on.

In fact, she thought, *I'll bet I have footprints all the way up my back.*

6

Something Fishy

"What a yukky way to spend a Sunday afternoon," Jean said.

She stared at the green slime on the side of the fishbowl. She and Belinda were supposed to take turns cleaning it. But Jean was the only one who seemed to have time.

In the bathroom Jean trapped the two fish with a small net. After putting them in a cup of water, she dumped the foul-smelling water down the sink. Using four paper towels, she scrubbed at the moldy build-up inside the fishbowl.

Downstairs the door bell rang. After a few seconds her mother called up the stairs. "Jean? Stacy's here."

Jean poked her head out the bathroom door. "Come on up, Stacy!" she yelled.

Soon two blonde fuzzy pigtails bobbed around the corner of the bathroom door. "Phew! It stinks in here. Smells like a swamp." Stacy wrinkled her turned-up nose as she perched on the edge of the tub.

"I know. But Albert and Francis couldn't see out through the scum." Jean rinsed the fishbowl and wiped the outside dry. "I don't want them to get sick or anything." She gazed fondly at the goldfish in the Mickey Mouse cup. Replacing the green marbles and plaster castle in the fishbowl, she filled it with clean water.

"My first turtle died," Stacy said matter-of-factly. "I kept forgetting to clean his bowl. I think he got some disease. His shell got soft and he smelled really rank." She pinched her nostrils shut. "I take better care of my new turtle, but I hate it. I'd even pay someone to clean his bowl every week."

"I know what you mean. It's a stinky job," Jean said. She netted a fish and scooped it up. It landed in the clean fish bowl with a soft plop. "At least Marshmallow won't smell like these fish."

Stacy nodded. "How much money have you saved?"

"Only four-fifty so far. I wish I knew a way to make more money."

"What about a paper route? Mine pays pretty well."

Jean shook her head firmly. "Not after subbing for you last week. I've had my fill of broken bike chains and crabby old ladies. I want something different." She squatted beside Stacy. "But what?"

Stacy twisted a pigtail around her finger. "My dad says the biggest money-makers in history were people who found a need and filled it."

"What's that mean?"

Stacy frowned. "It means to think of something that somebody needs. Like a person decided people would like to have someone wash their dishes. Presto! He invents the dishwasher. Or someone thought people would need rides around the city, so he invents taxis. Things like that."

"Maybe you're right."

Jean thought about what Stacy said as she placed Albert in the bowl with Francis. Her idea made sense. However, Jean couldn't think of a need to fill. Not one that people would pay for.

Jean and Stacy spent the rest of the afternoon sprawled across Jean's bed listening to records. Strumming imaginary guitars, they howled along with Jean's father's country western songs. They were limp from laughing by the time Stacy had to go home for supper.

That night, as Jean stood under the shower, Stacy's words again came to mind. "Find a need and fill it." But what?

She grabbed her towel and dried off briskly. As she squirted toothpaste on the toothbrush, she noticed the fishnet by the sink. Frowning, she turned on the electric toothbrush. Something buzzed around in the back of her mind, something she couldn't put her finger on.

And then all at once she did know what it was. Stacy had said she would gladly pay someone to clean Georgie's turtle bowl.

Maybe she was only kidding. But Jean was positive that she and Stacy weren't the only ones who hated cleaning fish and turtle bowls. Maybe other people would pay her to clean their filthy bowls. It would be a dirty job, but it might help her to bring Marshmallow home sooner.

On Monday Jean rushed home from school and went straight to her room. Hauling her art supplies out from under the bed, she found her brightest felt markers. She chewed her thumbnail. Finally she decided on the wording for her signs.

She lettered carefully on the posterboard:

"Attention Fish and Turtle Owners! !
Do you hate to clean your pet's bowl?
I will do it for you! !
Fish and turtle bowls—50¢.   Fishtanks—$1.00."

She leaned back and studied her sign. Then she added three bright orange fish, a green turtle and two more exclamation marks. Satisfied, she signed her name and phone number at the bottom. At the last minute she added in tiny letters: "Interested in homes near 422 E. 12th St." She didn't want customers from all over town. She couldn't spend all her time traveling back and forth.

The next day she carried three signs to school. She tacked one to the student bulletin board by the front door. She hoped her orange fish and green turtle attracted the kids' attention. She'd wanted to frame her sign with their flashing Christmas tree lights but her mom had flatly refused.

After school she stopped at Grason's Grocery and the Burger Palace. Both places were always jammed with customers. After getting permission, she taped her signs in their windows.

Full of hope, she hurried home. Now all she had to do was wait.

During supper the telephone rang. Belinda jumped up from the table. "I know it's for me," she claimed. "Rob and I have something important to talk over." She glided from the room.

In ten seconds she returned, a sour expression on her face. "It's for you, Jean," she said. Her eyes narrowed. "But make it short. I'm sure Rob is trying to call me at this very minute."

Holding her breath, Jean hurried from the room. Could her signs have produced some interest already? She took a deep breath and picked up the phone. "Yes? This is Jean."

"Hello. This is Mildred Thompkins. I live three blocks away from you. I saw your advertisement at the Burger Palace this evening. I would like to ask you about your services."

Jean grinned into the mouthpiece. "Well, I'm

interested in cleaning fish and turtle bowls and fish-tanks. I would pick up the bowls and bring them home to clean. That way I can clean several at once. I would, of course, clean a fishtank in your home." Mentally Jean scolded herself for her breathless voice. She wanted to sound like an experienced businesswoman.

"I have a small tank of exotic fish. My husband bought them, but leaves me to clean the tank." Mrs. Thompkins sounded aggrieved. "I think having it cleaned every other week should be sufficient. For a dollar, right?"

"That's right," Jean said briskly. "What day would be best for you?"

"How about starting a week from Thursday?" she asked. "About four o'clock?"

"That would be fine." Out of the corner of her eye, Jean saw Belinda tapping her foot impatiently. "What's your address?"

Jean wrote it down carefully on the pad by the phone. After thanking Mrs. Thompkins and hanging up, she jumped in the air. Her head hit the hanging lamp. It swung crazily, creating dancing shadows on the walls.

"My first customer!" Jean cried. "A lady wants me to clean her fishtank next Thursday. If I do a good job, I'll clean it every two weeks after that."

"How gross," Belinda said, curling her lip. "Anyway, what do you know about cleaning fishtanks?"

Jean opened her eyes wide. "What is there to know? I've cleaned Albert's and Francis's bowl a million times."

"That's hardly the same." Belinda tossed her hair over her shoulder. "What do you know about filters, hoses, tropical fish, or a proper ecological balance in an aquarium?"

For the first time Jean felt a twinge of doubt. Was it different to clean a fishtank than a fishbowl? Surely not, she decided. Belinda was just being mean because Rob hadn't called yet.

Pivoting on her heel, Jean marched out to the kitchen to tell her parents about the phone call.

By bedtime the telephone had rung for Jean two more times. Both calls had been students from school asking about her signs. She arranged to clean Stuart Mason's fishbowl and Jenny Little's turtle bowl each Friday after school.

Humming a spirited tune, she waltzed around the bedroom. Already she had three customers! She guessed other people hated cleaning fishbowls too.

"Can't you stop that croaking?" Belinda snapped as she trudged into the room. Her head sprouted tiny curlers, guaranteed to produce ringlets by morning. "It's enough to give a person a migraine."

Jean stopped in mid-hum. "Sorry," she mumbled.

Jean knew Rob hadn't called after all. Belinda looked furious. Having three customers call hadn't helped. Belinda had rushed to the telephone each time. And each time she'd glared as she called Jean to the phone.

The next day at school Stacy rushed up to Jean. "Guess what? I've found your first customer—me!" Her frizzy pigtails bobbed excitedly.

"What do you mean?"

"I talked to Mom last night. She said she'd be happy to pay you fifty cents to clean Georgie's turtle bowl. She gets tired of nagging me about it. I never seem to have time with my paper route."

"That's great!" Jean said. "But you're my fourth customer. I got three phone calls last night." She told Stacy about Mrs. Thompkin's tank and the turtle and fish bowls.

"Neat! It sounds like you're in business!"

"Thanks to your idea." Jean linked her arm through Stacy's as they filed into the school building. "It won't be long now before I bring Marshmallow home."

That night three calls resulted in two more customers. One tired-sounding mother wanted her fishtank cleaned every other Tuesday. An eighth-grade girl wanted her fishbowl cleaned every Friday. The third caller needed her turtle bowl cleaned. However, her home was ten blocks away. Jean intended to collect the bowls on Friday in Mark's wagon, and she didn't want to walk that far.

Curled up on the living room couch, Jean doodled on a piece of scratch paper. So far she had six customers. Four bowls cleaned every Friday would give her two dollars a week. Plus she had two fish-tanks to clean every other week. That would make another four dollars a month.

Jean knew there was four fifty upstairs in her money box. On Friday she would make two dollars cleaning fish and turtle bowls. On Saturday her father would give her three dollars for allowance and next week's school lunches. She added quickly. By Monday she would have nearly ten dollars! Her dream of bringing Marshmallow home didn't seem impossible anymore.

On Friday after school Jean jogged all the way home. Changing into cut-off jeans and a faded sweatshirt, she set off down the street with Mark's wagon. She clutched the list of addresses in her hand.

All four houses were in a six block area. At three places the dirty bowls had been emptied for her. But at Stuart's house three goldfish still swam lazily in their grimy bowl.

Stuart watched Jean net the fish, deposit them in a large glass, and dump the filthy water down the sink.

"Tell your Mom I'll have your bowl back in about an hour," Jean said. She wrapped it in an old bathtowel. Outside she stacked the bowl in the wagon and cushioned it with other bathtowels from her mother's rag bag.

On the way home she avoided the cracks and

humps in the sidewalk. She couldn't let the glass bowls bump against each other and break. At home she carried the filthy bowls, two at a time, up to the bathroom.

Jean decided to let the dirty bowls soak for ten minutes. While hot water splashed in the tub, she added a capful of bubblebath. The churning water foamed with bubbles. She dunked the bowls in the tub. They disappeared under a mountain of suds.

At that moment Belinda padded into the bathroom. "I *thought* I smelled bubblebath. How did you know I was going to take a bath? Rob and I are going to the Skate-arama tonight." She hugged Jean. "You're the sweetest! I'll bet no one else has a little sister who runs a bubblebath for them."

Jean squirmed at her words. "Actually, I didn't. Run you a bath, I mean."

"What are you talking about?" Belinda squinted. "Isn't that my bubblebath I smell? The bottle Rob gave me?"

"I just borrowed a little. I'm getting ready to wash four fish and turtle bowls. They're soaking in the tub so they'll be easier to clean."

"Get them *out!*" Belinda planted her feet wide apart, hands on hips. "And don't *ever* use my bubblebath again."

"Okay, okay," Jean mumbled. She glanced at her watch. The ten minutes were nearly up. "I'll take them out now."

"And scour that tub *immediately*. I won't have any fish scum floating in my bathwater." She flounced out of the bathroom with a loud sniff.

Jean rolled her eyes as she drained the tub. Belinda could sure be bossy, she thought. She'd make a great dictator someday.

Using paper towels, Jean scrubbed the first fishbowl. It was oval, with flower designs cut in the glass. It took a long time to get the dirt out of the tiny crevices. After that she moved on to the second bowl, the third, and finally the last bowl. A mound of moldy-smelling paper towels piled up beside the tub.

"Are you out of the bathroom yet?" Belinda yelled down the hall.

"Almost." Jean put a bowl under the tub faucet to rinse. The water gushed out. When it hit the bowl, it splashed all over the wall. Green flecks of scum and gray-green froth clung to the white bathroom wall.

Groaning, Jean finished rinsing the bowls. She was horrified as she noticed the time. She had planned to have the bowls delivered fifteen minutes ago.

After wiping down the wall and rinsing the tub, Jean carried the four sparkling bowls downstairs. She placed them gently in the wagon and started down the sidewalk.

Later, after collecting her two dollars, she headed home. She hoped cleaning the bowls didn't take so long next week. But even if they did, Jean felt it was worth it. In two weeks at the most, she would be able to bring Marshmallow home. She couldn't wait.

7

Mark's Surprise

That weekend Jean checked out three books from the library about the proper care of dogs. She studied for hours about nutrition and dog training techniques. She wanted Marshmallow to be healthy and well-behaved. *Her* dog wasn't going to chase cars and bite mailmen.

After school on Monday Jean pedaled out to the Goldridge Animal Shelter. Once again the waiting room was empty. Instead of ringing the service bell, Jean poked her head through the open door behind the counter.

Mr. Sorensen hummed a tuneless melody as he fed the cats in the middle room. Jean watched him stroke each cat and kitten before closing its cage.

For a man with such huge hands, she was surprised how gentle he was.

"Hi, Mr. Sorensen." She spoke timidly. "Can I visit Marshmallow today?"

Mr. Sorensen glanced over his shoulder. "Hi, Jean. You sure can. I'll take you back there in just a minute."

"There's no hurry." Jean came further into the room. "Can I help you?" She peered into each cage holding kittens.

"I'm afraid the only job left is replacing the dirty newspaper in the cages," he said, laughing. "I don't think it's a job you'd enjoy."

"I don't mind." She motioned to a stack of old papers. "Are those the ones you use?"

When Mr. Sorensen nodded, Jean sat down on the floor and began tearing the newspapers into strips. Soon she had a huge mound of shredded paper. "What cage shall I start with?" she asked.

"Any cage is fine. Use this little shovel to scrape the soiled papers into that box. When the box gets full, dump it in the garbage can outside. It's through that side door," he said, pointing.

Jean took the shovel and opened the door of the first cage. A placid tiger cat stared at her with glassy green eyes. "What do I do with this cat while I clean the cage?"

"You can put her in that empty cage over there."

Jean scratched the cat behind its ear, then gently picked her up. The striped cat nestled into the crook of her arm and began to purr. The vibration tickled Jean's skin.

After putting the cat in the empty cage, Jean shoveled the dirty paper into the box. She tried not to breathe. She hadn't known it would be such a stinky job. She tossed handfuls of clean newspaper inside and returned the striped cat to her cage. The tiger cat rolled over on its back and purred. Jean grinned and scratched its stomach, then closed her cage door.

"I wish someone would take her home. I bet she'd like to run around free," Jean said. She wiggled her fingers through the wire of the cage.

Mr. Sorensen turned from feeding the kittens. "That's one of the hardest things about working here. You hate to see the animals locked up." He pointed to the next cage. "Some animals, like that tabby, fight when you try to put them back in. Watch him when you open his cage."

Jean nodded and unhooked the cage door. The cat lunged forward and pressed its nose through the crack. Before Jean could stop him, he had thrust the cage door open two more inches. With a soft thump he jumped to the floor.

"Oh, no!" Jean dashed after the cat. He disappeared behind the large bags of cat and dog food piled in the corner. She peered behind the sacks. Two glowing green eyes stared back at her from a dark space between the bags.

Jean reached into the small space. As her fingers closed around his body, he slithered out of her grasp. Slinking sideways, he disappeared again.

Jean crouched down on her hands and knees and clicked her tongue. "Come here. Come on out," she coaxed.

Mr. Sorensen chuckled and knelt beside her. In his hand were three kitty biscuits shaped like fish. "Here. Hold these out to him. They're his favorite snack. You can usually lure him out with these."

Jean took the biscuits. She held one in her open palm. "Come out now. Look what I have for you."

In less than fifteen seconds the tabby poked his nose out. It twitched. Jean gave him the fish snack, then moved back a few inches. As soon as the cat finished his first biscuit, he crept out a little further and took the second snack. When he reached for the third one, Jean grabbed his collar.

Mr. Sorensen applauded. Jean grinned as she carried the wriggling cat to the empty cage.

She scooped out four more cages before she emptied the box into the trash can outside. By this time Mr. Sorensen was done feeding the cats. Together he and Jean cleaned the rest of the cages.

The time passed quickly for Jean as they talked about each of the cats. She discovered that many of the stray animals were brought in by strangers. These were for adoption. Others, like the sleek black tom cat Jean held, were "boarders." Their owners were on vacation. The animal shelter was paid to care for them during that time.

"Money from the boarders helps the shelter a lot," Mr. Sorensen said. "It's expensive to care for stray animals."

"I think you take really good care of them. But I can't wait to take Marshmallow home where she can run around our fenced-in back yard," Jean said. "It won't be long now. I have nearly ten dollars saved." She explained about her new cleaning business.

Mr. Sorensen congratulated her as they walked back to the dog room. When he opened Marshmallow's cage, the puppy bounded straight into Jean's arms.

"She knows me!" Jean cried. "Don't you think so, Mr. Sorensen?"

"Absolutely sure of it," he agreed. "Keep calling her by her new name. By the time she goes home with you, she'll answer to Marshmallow."

"I'll do that." Jean stroked the plump animal. "Can I stay and play with her awhile?"

"Sure. Holler when you're ready to go." Mr. Sorensen sauntered back toward the front of the building.

After the door closed Jean bent over her puppy. "Did you know that your name is Marshmallow? You're going to come home with me soon." She scratched softly behind Marshmallow's ear. "I'll fix a warm doghouse for you to live in. I'll always feed you healthy food. When it's summer vacation, we'll play together all the time."

The puppy stared at her as if she understood every word. At least Jean liked to think so. She seemed like such a smart puppy.

"Now I don't want you to think it's going to be all playtime at our house." Jean spoke as if to a small child. "You'll have to learn all kinds of things, like manners and obedience. I'm reading all about it so I can help you learn."

"I hope you mean that. Most kids don't know how to take proper care of animals."

The stern voice behind Jean startled her. She whirled around. Brent Davis stood a few cages away.

"Uh, hi. I didn't hear you come in," she stammered.

"I didn't mean to sneak up on you." Brent Davis held up his small black bag. "Mr. Sorensen asked me to check a stray dog brought in this morning."

Jean looked away in embarrassment. She patted Marshmallow's wet nose. "I guess it sounded dumb, talking to a puppy like that."

Brent Davis hesitated, then walked closer. "It's not dumb." He squatted down beside her and stroked Marshmallow's back. "It shows you love animals. They enjoy it when you talk to them."

Brent's friendlier tone of voice surprised Jean. "Is that why you became a vet? Because you love animals?"

"That's part of it." His eyebrows drew together

in a frown. "I grew up on a farm and watched too many sick animals die. I wanted to be able to do something, but couldn't." He brushed his unruly hair back from his face.

"Do you like being a vet?"

The frown disappeared. "I love it. Or I wouldn't do it."

Jean cuddled Marshmallow close. "Maybe I'll be a vet someday too. I love animals."

"There's more to it than that," Brent said. "There are years of hard work and training. Liking people doesn't make you a doctor. Loving animals doesn't make you a veterinarian."

"Maybe I could watch you work sometime." Jean cocked her head to one side. "That reminds me. Did the dog you examined last week have rabies?"

"No, but it did have a virus. Animals are subject to illnesses just like humans."

Mr. Sorensen poked his head through the door. "Ready for me to put Marshmallow back yet?" he called.

Jean glanced at her watch and gasped. "I had no idea it was almost five o'clock!" She scrambled to her feet. "Yes, I'd better have you put the puppy back." She gave Marshmallow one last squeeze while Mr. Sorensen opened the cage door. "See you next week, girl."

With a wave, Jean hurried down the long hallway to the waiting room. Dashing outside, she jumped on her bike and pedaled at top speed toward home. She had to fix supper before her parents got home.

Arriving out of breath, Jean took the stairs two at a time. She ran to her bedroom to change clothes. What she saw from the doorway made her skid to a halt.

Belinda posed in front of the full-length mirror, patting her hair. Her *pink* hair.

"What have you done?" Jean shrieked.

Belinda twirled around several times. "Isn't it wild? I dyed it to match my pink jeans. Now I'm a *real* strawberry blonde." She fluffed out her pink-streaked hair. "Rob and I are going skating again tonight at the roller rink."

For the first time Jean noticed the wet towels deposited around their bedroom. Some of them had pink stains on them. "Mom will never let you out in public looking like that."

Belinda smirked. "I called her at work and told her I ate early. Rob is picking me up at five-thirty. I'll be gone before Mom and Dad get home."

The ringing of the doorbell interrupted them. Peeking out their bedroom window, Jean saw Rob's bike parked in front. "He's here already."

"Wait a minute! You can't leave these towels all over. Mom will kill you if they stain the carpet." Jean knew she sounded like a nag, but she didn't care.

"Jeannie, be a doll," Belinda pleaded. "Clean up this mess before Mom gets home, okay?" She started down the hall. "And throw all those towels in the washing machine." Her footsteps echoed on the stairs.

Jean fumed as she surveyed the bedroom. If she didn't share the room with Belinda, she wouldn't pick up the mess. But it was her room too. She didn't want pink stains on the beige carpet. Grudgingly, she picked up the soggy towels and carried them down to the basement.

As she loaded the washer, she remembered her grandmother's comment. "You shouldn't allow yourself to be walked on," she'd said. Jean supposed she was right, but her grandmother didn't understand how Belinda behaved.

Since Belinda had already eaten, there were only four at the supper table that night. Jean munched her tacos in silence. Her mind was on her conversation with Brent Davis. The more she considered it, the more she wanted to be a vet someday.

Glancing up, she noticed a curious look pass between Mark and her father.

"What's going on?" Jean asked. "Did I miss something?"

Her father grinned and pushed back his chair. "Mark and I have something to show you outside when you're finished." He sounded mysterious.

"I'm finished now," Jean said. She dropped the rest of her taco. "What's outside?"

"You'll *never* guess," Mark said. He skipped to

the back door. Jean and her father followed close on his heels.

Outside they marched to a place behind the garage. Mark and his father stood there and grinned.

Jean threw up her hands in impatience. "Well? What do you have to show me?"

"Actually, it's Mark's surprise," her father said.

Mark knelt by a boxlike shape covered with an old blanket. "It's under here," he said. "You won't laugh anymore when I say I want to be a sanitation servant."

He whisked off the old blanket. Underneath was a doghouse! It looked like brand new. Over the door of the doghouse was painted the name "Marshmallow."

Jean gasped. "Where did you get this?" she asked, peering inside.

"I told Joe to keep his eyes open for dog stuff, even though you didn't want me to." Mark puffed out his chest importantly. "The Martins live three blocks away. When their dog got sick and died, they decided not to get another pet. Joe said he'd take their doghouse since they didn't know what to do with it. They were glad for Joe to haul it away."

"But it looks like new!"

"Dad did that," Mark said. "He painted it with some leftover yellow paint. Now it matches the house."

"I can't believe it." Jean shook her head. "This is just perfect. Thank you both."

Jean's father disappeared into the garage. He returned with a sack in his hand. "Joe also got this from the Martins." He handed the sack to Jean.

Inside the sack was a blue dog dish. It looked a little chewed on, but not too badly. It would be fine for feeding Marshmallow, Jean thought, at least until she could afford a new one.

Jean smiled down at her little brother. "When I bring Marshmallow home, you can play with her whenever you want. I'll even let you feed her sometimes."

Mark beamed. "That'd be neat!"

Jean put the dog dish inside the doghouse, then covered it again with the blanket. Humming softly, she followed her brother and father back into the house. Jean felt as though things were finally looking up. She had nearly ten dollars saved, her cleaning business was going well, she had a doghouse and dish. . . .

One more thing would make her day complete. She couldn't wait to see her parents' faces when Belinda walked in with pink hair.

8

Promises, Promises

That night Jean studied halfheartedly at the top of the stairs, with one ear listening for the front door. When Belinda came home at eight-thirty, Jean saw her tiptoe across the front hall toward the stairs.

"BELINDA!"

Jean cringed at her father's shocked voice. She peeked over the bannister as Belinda froze, shrugged, then turned and headed for the living room.

"Belinda!" their mother cried. "What have you done to your hair?"

"It'll wash out, Mom," Belinda assured her smoothly. "I'll go shampoo it out right now."

"Just a minute," her father interrupted. "How could you go out in public like that? It looks—it looks . . ." At that point, words failed him.

"I know it's a bit of a shock," Belinda said in a soothing voice. "But it's harmless. Really, Daddy."

Jean shook her head. She pictured Belinda sitting on the arm of her father's chair. She'd smile, making sure to deepen each dimple, then pat her father's cheek and be forgiven. Jean was totally unprepared for her mother's next words.

"That's really beside the point, Belinda," her mother said. "You knew we wouldn't have let you leave the house with your hair colored pink. So you disappeared before we got home and saw you. For being sneaky, you will no longer be allowed to go out on school evenings. We will expect you home every night during the week."

"But, Mom . . ."

"No buts."

"Dad?"

After a short pause, he answered. "You heard your mother. I agree with her."

Jean held her breath and listened, but nothing else was said. Scooting into the bathroom to brush her teeth, Jean couldn't help feeling that Belinda deserved the punishment. But she was going to hate having to be home in the evenings. If she'd been hard to live with *before,* she was going to be even worse now.

Jean crawled into bed before Belinda came upstairs. Her older sister was sure to blame her for being grounded. She'd never believe that Jean hadn't said a word to their parents about her hair. Jean pulled the covers over her head, intending to avoid Belinda for as long as possible.

After school Wednesday Jean walked home alone. Trudging up the stairs to her bedroom, she hummed tunelessly. As she reached the bedroom door, she stopped short. She couldn't believe her eyes.

Belinda flitted around like a butterfly as she picked up scattered shoes and clothes. She straightened the spreads on their twin beds and polished the mirrors above both dressers. Spotting Jean in the mirror's reflection, Belinda turned with a wide smile.

Jean came slowly into the room. "What are you doing?" she asked.

"What does it look like? I'm cleaning our room." Belinda dusted the bookcase and windowsill. "It's partly my responsibility. I know I'm not always much help."

"Things *were* looking pretty bad," Jean admitted. She tossed her books on the bed. "Thanks for cleaning up." She grabbed her worn jeans and sweater and changed her clothes.

Belinda hung Jean's skirt and blouse on padded hangers.

"You don't have to do that," Jean protested. She wondered what had come over her sister.

"Oh, that's all right." She examined Jean's blouse. "Say, would you like to wear my new blue sweater to school tomorrow? You don't have many new clothes."

"Your *new sweater*? I can't believe you'd let me."

Jean's eyes narrowed to slits as she studied her sister. "What's going on here anyway? What do you want from me?"

"Whatever are you talking about?" Belinda opened her blue eyes wide. Her lower lip protruded.

"I'm talking about all this housecleaning and lending me your new sweater. What's up?"

Belinda pulled loose threads from her dust cloth. "Nothing much. *Really*. I only wanted to ask you a *tiny* favor."

"I thought so." Jean braced herself for the tiny favor.

Belinda sighed wistfully. "You know the MORP is coming up soon. Rob is taking me," she said. "But I need some new sandals. Browne's Shoe Store is having a sale on sandals. It only lasts one more day."

"So why don't you buy some?" Jean asked, nonchalantly, already fairly sure of the answer.

"I'm a little short on cash. I spent most of my money on those pink jeans." She looked down at the carpet. Her long lashes rested on her creamy skin.

"Why don't you ask Mom for the money? Or better yet, Dad? He never says 'no' to you."

"When I bought the jeans, Mom said not to ask for another dime." Belinda glanced up. Her eyes flashed angrily. "She even told Dad not to lend me any money."

Jean refused to feel any sympathy for her sister. "What do you want from me?"

Belinda took a deep breath and leaned forward. "I wondered if you could possibly lend me the money you've saved for your puppy." Belinda patted her blue sweater, as if to remind Jean of her generous offer.

"Not on your life!" Jean shook her head firmly. "I've worked hard for that money. In another couple weeks I'll be able to bring Marshmallow home."

"Wait a minute! You still could. Just listen." Belinda moved and sat close to Jean on her bed. "I already have two babysitting jobs lined up for this weekend. After working Friday and Saturday nights I'll make more than the nine dollars I need." She took a deep breath. "But the sale only lasts one more day. You see, I only need the loan for a *mere* three days. After Saturday night I can pay it all back."

"I don't know," Jean mumbled. It didn't sound like much of a risk. Not if she would be paid back in three days. Still, Jean hated to part with her money. She'd eaten a lot of peanut butter sandwiches the last two weeks in order to save it.

"Please?" Belinda begged. Her big blue eyes filled with unshed tears.

Jean sighed inwardly. "I guess so." She reached under her bed for the tin Band-Aid box. She counted out nine dollars and paused. Grudgingly, she handed it to Belinda.

Belinda gave her a quick squeeze. "Thanks, Jeannie. I knew I could count on you." She tucked the money in her purse and sauntered from the room.

"Remember, you promised to repay me this weekend!" Jean called after her.

Already she regretted lending her money to Belinda. She stared at the dollar and two quarters left in the box. The quarters clinked as Jean pushed the nearly empty box back under her bed. At least the next day she would earn another dollar to add to the box.

After school Thursday Jean consulted the scrap of paper she'd stuck in her math book. Today she was to clean her second fishtank. She read the scribbled address Mrs. Thompkins had given her on the phone.

The house was easy to find. Jean took a deep breath and rang the door bell. She heard a TV blaring when Mrs. Thompkins opened the door.

"Hello. Can I help you?" the young woman asked. She looked trim in her matching slacks and sweater.

"I'm Jean Harvey. You called last week about your fishtank. I'm supposed to clean it today." Although her knees wobbled, she hoped she sounded confident.

"Oh, yes. Come in." She held the door open for Jean. "I'm rather busy right now. I'll show you where everything is before I get back to work."

Mrs. Thompkins led the way through the living room where a small boy stared at cartoons. Jean followed her to the large kitchen. A huge hexagonal-shaped fishtank stood below the kitchen window. It was across the room from the sink, and still full of fish and murky water.

"There's the tank," Mrs. Thompkins said. "And here are all the cleaners and brushes and the hose and bucket you'll need. I understand you have experience cleaning tanks?"

"Um, yes. In fact, I just cleaned one two days ago for a customer."

"Fine. I'll leave you to your work. If you need anything, I'll be in the bedroom at the end of the hall. I'm sewing a costume for my daughter's dance recital."

Mrs. Thompkins smiled absentmindedly and hurried from the room. Almost immediately Jean heard the whir of the sewing machine.

Jean's smile faded as she stared at the huge fishtank. Then she gazed at the bewildering collection of cleaning equipment. What she had told Mrs. Thompkins was true. She *had* cleaned another tank on Tuesday. But it had been nothing like that monstrosity across the room.

On Tuesday the tank had been the size of a small aquarium. Before Jean had arrived at the house, the woman had removed the tropical fish and plastic plants. She'd also drained the dirty water. All Jean had had to do was scrub the inside and outside of the glass tank. It had taken her barely half an hour.

But *this* tank was something else. The murky

water bubbled and boiled as giant goldfish swam around the tank. A fluorescent light above the tank illuminated only the top five inches of cloudy water. Peering behind the tank, Jean grew more confused by the array of hoses, filters and pumps. She had absolutely no idea where to begin.

"Unplug it."

Jean whirled around. The small boy from the living room stood behind her. He rocked back and forth on the balls of his feet. His hands were pushed deep into his pockets.

"What did you say?" she asked.

"Unplug it." He motioned to the electrical outlet near the floor. "Then take the light off the top."

Embarrassed, Jean decided it was probably a good idea. She should have thought of it by herself. She pulled the plug from the outlet, then carefully lifted the light off the tank. She laid it on the round oak table.

Studying the back of the tank, she pointed to a compartment containing a dirty pillow-shaped thing. "Do you know what this is?" she whispered. Jean was careful to keep her voice low. She couldn't let Mrs. Thompkins hear her asking advice from her little boy.

"It's a filter."

"Oh." Jean unhooked the plastic compartment and carried it to the sink. In a box on the counter she found a clean filter. She threw the dirty one away and rinsed out the plastic compartment. Putting in a new filter, she turned and smiled at the boy. This wasn't so hard after all.

Next she lifted off the glass lid and carried it carefully to the sink. She washed and wiped it dry. Then she pulled out the plastic pipe used to aerate the water. She rinsed it under the faucet.

Her confidence mounting, Jean returned to the fishtank. She dropped to her hands and knees and examined the bottom of the tank.

Now what? she wondered.

There were no rollers or wheels on the tank. How could she move it to the sink to dump the dirty water? And there was no net to catch the fish. Was she supposed to grab them with her bare hands? she wondered. Jean shuddered at the thought.

She squatted beside the small boy. Peering into his solemn face, she asked, "What's your name?"

"Tommy. I'm four years old."

"Well, Tommy, you seem to know all about cleaning fishtanks." Jean paused and listened closely. With relief she heard the sewing machine still humming softly.

Tommy puffed out his chest. "I watch Mom clean it all the time. It's easy."

"Good. How does your mother get the fish out before she dumps the dirty water?" Jean was alarmed at the hint of desperation in her voice. She forced herself to smile.

"She doesn't."

"What do you mean, she doesn't?" Jean thought

her question wasn't clear. "She must take out the fish. Otherwise they will die when the water is dumped out."

Tommy stubbornly shook his head back and forth. Jean decided he was certainly a child of few words.

Jean frowned. "But doesn't she take out all the water?"

"Nope. Only down to here." Tommy pointed to a spot four inches from the bottom.

Jean suddenly understood. This must be the ecological balance that Belinda had mentioned. Jean watched as Tommy brought her a green plastic bucket.

"Here."

"Uh, thanks."

Jean decided she was supposed to use the bucket to dip out the dirty water. But when she tried to put the bucket in the tank, she found it wouldn't fit. The hexagonal shape of the tank made it impossible.

"Suck it out."

Jean gasped and whirled around. "*What* did you say?"

Tommy handed her a piece of rubber hose about six feet long. One end of the hose had a large rubber cup attached. Pointing to the cup, Tommy said, "Put that end in the water."

Jean was skeptical, but she dropped the cup end of the hose into the tank. The heavy end sank to the bottom. About four feet of hose hung out over the side.

Tommy pointed to the skinny end. "Suck it," he said again.

Now Jean knew what he meant. A siphon. After sucking on the rubber hose, the dirty water would begin to flow into the bucket. *That* was how Mrs. Thompkins emptied the tank.

Jean knelt beside the tank and peered into the murky water. Then she reached into the tank to remove the plastic plants. Swishing her hand through the water, she found three plants and a plaster sculpture of a coral reef. As she picked up the reef, a fish swam past her hand. Its tail brushed her fingers. She shivered and jerked her hand from the water.

Tommy stared silently while Jean filled one side of the kitchen sink with soapy water. The plastic plants and plaster reef were put in to soak.

"How are you coming?" Mrs. Thompkins called from down the hall.

Jean smiled brightly at Tommy, praying he wouldn't open his mouth. "Everything's fine," she said.

She held her breath until she heard Mrs. Thompkins's sewing machine start up again. Sighing with relief, she turned to the fishtank. She had put it off as long as possible. Tommy watched her through narrowed eyes.

"Would you like to suck on this hose?" Jean wheedled. "I'll bet it's lots of fun."

"Yuk."

Yuk was right, Jean thought. But she knew it had

to be done. Maybe if she were quick, she wouldn't get any of the filthy water in her mouth.

Jean wiped the end of the hose on her jeans. Trying not to gag, she put it in her mouth and sucked gently. Yanking it out, she stuck the hose down into the bucket. She waited hopefully. Not a drop appeared.

She tried again, sucking a little harder. Whipping it from her mouth, she stuck the end into the bucket again. Still no water came from the hose. Tommy shook his head in disgust.

Taking a deep breath, she put the hose in her mouth one more time. She sucked sharply. Just as she started to put the hose in the bucket, water squirted into her mouth. She spit the foul-tasting liquid into the bucket. Her stomach heaved and lurched. Jean forced herself to breathe deeply.

Tommy grabbed the hose and pushed it down into the bucket. A trickle turned into a steady stream. Dirty water slowly filled the bucket. When the bucket was nearly full, suddenly the flow stopped.

"*Now* what?" Jean muttered. She stared at the tank.

"Clogged." Tommy pointed to the rubber cup on the end of the hose.

"Oh. Great." Jean reached in and shook the colored gravel from the end of the hose. Immediately the water flowed again. When the bucket was full, Jean lifted the large end out of the water. The water dwindled to a trickle.

Jean carried the heavy bucket to the sink. Cautiously she poured the contents down the empty half of the sink. Bracing herself, she went back to refill the bucket. This time she had no trouble getting the water to flow.

After Jean had lugged the full bucket to the sink six more times, her arms ached. Nearly an hour had passed. She hadn't even started cleaning the tank yet. With one eye on the clock, she swished the plastic plants through the soapy water. When she rinsed them off, she was pleased they looked clean.

With handfuls of paper towels, she scrubbed the inside of the tank. The slime came off easily. Then she polished the fingerprints from the outside of the glass.

Her shoulders sagged as Jean carried buckets of clean water to refill the tank. She replaced the plastic plants and coral reef. The filter, the light, and the aerating hose were hooked up next. Finally she covered the tank with the glass lid and plugged in the light.

Jean crouched beside the gleaming tank. Bright orange fish swam between clean plants. Sparkling bubbles rose through the water to the surface.

Jean rubbed her forehead tiredly. Cleaning the tank was harder work than she had expected. But that didn't really matter to her. The important thing was that she was a dollar closer to bringing Marshmallow home.

9

Super Scrubber

Jean rolled over wearily and let her book drop to the floor. Lying in bed made her so tired. She'd done nothing all weekend except sleep, drink chicken broth and read.

Having the flu always left her feeling limp and wrung out. But, she admitted, that was better than how she'd felt on Friday after cleaning those fish and turtle bowls.

Jean heard a car purr to a stop outside. That was followed by the slam of a door and loud "good-bye."

Belinda must be home, Jean thought. *It's about time.*

Jean had barely seen Belinda all weekend. She had babysat both Friday and Saturday nights, as she had promised. Then that afternoon she'd disappeared to study with her best friend, Cheryl Midden.

Jean had been too sick all weekend to think of anything but keeping her broth down. She hadn't even thought about the nine dollars Belinda owed her. But now she intended to collect. As soon as Belinda came upstairs, she'd demand her money.

After what seemed like a long time, Belinda padded up the stairs in her bare feet. She tiptoed into their bedroom. When she saw Jean was up, she dropped her books with a clatter.

"You awake?" she asked. "How do you feel?"

Jean propped herself up on her elbows. "A lot better. I think I'll go to school tomorrow."

"Good," Belinda said absentmindedly. She picked up her robe and pajamas and headed for the door. "Guess I'll take my bath now."

"Wait a minute. I'd like you to repay that loan now. Before you forget." Jean pulled her money box out from under the bed. After cleaning bowls on Friday, plus her allowance and food money, she had over six dollars in the box.

Belinda shrugged, her robe draped over her shoulder. "Can't it wait a little while? I'd like to get cleaned up while the bathroom is empty."

"It'll only take a minute." Jean narrowed her eyes and frowned. "What's the matter? You *did* babysit both nights, didn't you?"

"Of course I did. I made twelve dollars altogether." Belinda hesitated, then came back into the room. She twisted the button on her robe. "The truth is, I have a little problem."

"*What* problem?" Jean felt an ominous sense of misgiving. "Didn't you get paid?"

"Yes, I got paid. But Rob's birthday is next week . . ." She slumped down on Jean's bed, sighing and fluttering her long lashes. "He bought me such a great present on my birthday. I *have* to get him something nice."

"Oh, no, you don't." Jean shook her head firmly. "You have to repay me first. You promised."

"Well, I can't," Belinda snapped, standing up. "I went shopping this afternoon with Cheryl and bought Rob a present. It's a tape—his favorite group." She pulled the small package from her purse and held it out to show Jean.

Jean slapped it away. "You had no right! That was *my* money you spent!"

"Keep your voice down." Belinda hurried to the door and closed it. "I didn't spend all twelve dollars. I'll give you what I have left plus the money from my next sitting job." She rummaged in the bottom of her purse and handed Jean two wrinkled dollar bills.

"Two dollars is all you have left?" Jean waved the bills in Belinda's face. "You owe me *nine*. Just wait till Mom hears about this." She swung her legs over the side of the bed.

"No! Don't! Wait a minute," Belinda begged.

"You don't know what it's like. You're just a little kid." She paced around the room, her arms flung out dramatically. "Rob would think I was really cheap if I got him some dumb little present. It just isn't done that way."

"I don't care. That was *my* money you spent— money I've been saving to bring my puppy home." Jean pointed an accusing finger at her sister. "You could have saved your own money. What if *I* think you're really cheap!"

Belinda took Jean's arm and pulled her over to the bed. "Let's sit down and talk about this calmly."

"I don't want to talk about it calmly! I want my money!"

"I have an idea." Belinda twisted her hair around her finger. "If you give me just one more week, I'm sure I could repay the other seven dollars. Just one week. Please!"

Jean glared at her sister's pleading face. She wished Belinda wouldn't beg. It made her somehow feel guilty.

Why do I always have to be the one to understand? Jean thought angrily. *Why do I always have to give in?*

Jean poked her finger in Belinda's stomach. "One week? You think you can have the money by next Sunday?"

"I'm sure I can. I'll babysit again. I'll do extra jobs for Mom. Just give me a week. If I don't have the money for you next Sunday, you can tell Mom and Dad then." Belinda cocked her head to one side. "Well?"

"I guess so," Jean mumbled. She crawled back into bed. "One week. And that's all. No more excuses."

Belinda breathed a loud sigh of relief. "Thanks, Jeannie. If there's anything I can ever do for you, let me know." With an airy wave, she picked up her robe and headed down the hall.

Jean stuck out her tongue at the closed door. *Talk about empty offers,* she thought and flopped back on her pillows.

The week passed quickly. Jean regained her strength, but was grateful that it wasn't the week to clean fishtanks.

When the last bell rang on Friday, Jean scooped up her school books. She dodged around kids and rushed toward the door. She wanted to get her four fish and turtle bowls cleaned right away. Stacy had invited her to go swimming at the Y that evening, and Jean really wanted to go. She felt as if she'd done nothing but work, work, work for a long time.

As Jean reached the door, she heard her name called.

"Can you wait a minute, Jean?" Miss Brookner said. "And you, too, Stuart and John."

Stacy paused beside Jean at the door. "What's up?"

"I don't know." Jean shrugged as she watched her teacher. "I hope this doesn't take long. I want to get those bowls cleaned so we can go swimming."

Stacy nodded rapidly, her pigtails bobbing. "I can't wait! This has been a long week." She waved as she left. "When I finish my paper route I'll call you."

Jean made a circle with her thumb and first finger. "I'll hurry." She joined Stuart, John and Miss Brookner at a table at the back of the room.

Miss Brookner placed several stacks of colored construction paper on the long table. "If you three kids have time, I could use some help this afternoon. As you know, our spring Open House is Monday night. Your parents will be visiting our room." She glanced at the bare walls. "It wouldn't hurt if we decorated a bit."

Stuart pushed his glasses up on his sweaty nose. "Will this take long? I'm meeting the guys at the park in an hour."

"That's fine. We should be done before that. In any case, you can leave anytime you need to." Miss Brookner smiled at them. "I knew I could count on each of you to help. You're all such good workers." She pushed back her chair. "What I need done is this. While I fix a 'welcome' bulletin board, I want you to paste these compositions onto the colored paper. Then we'll put them up around the room for the parents to read."

Jean groaned inwardly at the large pile of stories on the table. She glanced at the clock. Already it was three forty-five. She honestly didn't have the time to spare, she thought.

But Miss Brookner had already started on the bulletin board, and Stuart and John sorted through the stories. Jean didn't see how she could be the only one to leave.

Determined to hurry, she picked up the red and yellow paper and a handful of stories. With quick jabs, she dabbed paste on the corners of the first story. Centering it on red paper, she slammed her fist down on each corner to stick it on tight.

Miss Brookner stopped and turned to Jean. "Is anything wrong?" she asked.

Jean glanced up in remorse. She hadn't meant to hit the paper so hard. "No, nothing's wrong." She forced a smile and grabbed a second story.

Mentally she scolded herself. *Why didn't I say I have a job after school? What does it matter if Stuart and John stay but I don't? Why does it matter so much what Miss Brookner thinks of me?*

Sitting stooped over, Jean felt her neck cramp. She rubbed the knotted muscles at the back of her neck. She'd been hunched over her paste jar for twenty minutes, she realized. It was already after four o'clock.

Her stomach churned as she recalled how long it would take to collect her fish and turtle bowls, clean them and return them. Of all nights to run late. It was her night to fix supper too. And she knew if supper was late she could forget about swimming at the Y.

Just before four-thirty, Jean finished pasting her last story on yellow construction paper. "If that's all, I need to leave now," Jean said.

Miss Brookner paused in hanging streamers from the lights to the windows. "Thank you so much for helping, Jean. I really appreciate it. See you on Monday." She twisted the streamer and taped it in place.

Jean grabbed her books. She trotted down the hall and out the door. Outside she broke into a run. After two blocks a stitch in her side forced her to a stop. Bent over, she clutched her side.

Panting, she half-walked, half-jogged the rest of the way home. She dumped her books on the front porch, grabbed Mark's wagon, and turned back the way she had come.

The wagon rattled behind her as she dragged it down the bumpy sidewalk. Within fifteen minutes she collected three bowls. Rushing on, she winced at the clinking glass when the wagon hit some rough cement.

At the fourth house the woman complained that she was late. Jean barely heard the woman because her head was splitting with a rotten headache. After promising to have Mrs. Little's turtle bowl back within the hour, she hurried home as fast as the bouncing glass bowls would allow.

When she arrived it was nearly five o'clock. She had barely an hour to scrub the four bowls, return them to her customers, race home and fix supper. Jean's temples throbbed as she took the stairs two at a time.

Jean wished she had time to soak the filthy bowls. She'd just have to scrub harder, she decided. And *faster*.

Three of the bowls were still sticky with wet slime. But the fourth one was totally dry, the green scum turned brown. *It must have been emptied early today,* Jean thought. She decided to let it soak and scour it last.

She attacked the sediment around the first turtle bowl. It reminded Jean of a miniature bathtub ring. Slowly the green line disappeared as she worked her way around the glass. One crumpled paper towel followed another into the wastebasket.

A sharp knock on the bathroom door startled Jean. "Who is it?"

"It's me!" Belinda called. "Come out of the bathroom right now!"

Throwing down her paper towel, Jean yanked open the door. "I can't come out yet. I'm not finished."

Belinda glanced around the bathroom in disgust. Dirty fishbowls sat on the back and seat of the pink toilet. Filthy green paper towels overflowed the wastebasket. A foul odor hovered in the air.

"P-U! Does this stuff have to stink so bad?" She sprayed pine scent air freshener around the room. "Whether you're finished or not, I need to take a bath. *Right now.* Have you forgotten? The MORP is tonight. If I don't take my bath now, I won't be ready when Rob gets here."

"I'll hurry, but I have to finish. I have less than an hour to return these bowls." Jean pushed aside the ceramic container of toothbrushes by the sink and resumed her scrubbing.

"But what about me?" Belinda wailed.

"Go ahead and take your bath. I won't watch." Jean rinsed the turtle bowl and dried it out.

"I will *not* have an audience for my bath." Belinda folded her arms across her chest. "Can't a person have a little privacy around here?"

"I'm doing the best I can," Jean said between clenched teeth.

Belinda glared at her for a full minute. Finally she asked, "How long will it take you to finish?"

"Half an hour at least."

"Half an hour! That doesn't leave me nearly enough time to get ready!"

Jean pointed to the three filthy bowls waiting to be cleaned. "You could help me finish. I'd get done in half the time." She scratched her nose. "I'd deduct fifty cents from your loan for every bowl you cleaned."

"You must be kidding!" Belinda held up her beautifully painted fingernails. "Get that green slime under these nails? It would never come out. I won't dance at the MORP with green fingernails." She flounced down the hall.

Jean kicked the door shut and picked up the second bowl. Ripping a paper towel off the roll, she saw they were nearly gone. She made each towel last as long as she could. She scoured with them until they shredded. She tried scraping the dirt off with her thumbnail but she made slow progress.

Jean glanced at her watch. Five thirty-five. And she wasn't half done. She pressed her hands over her ears. Closing her eyes tight, she listened to the dull *thud-thud* as blood pounded in her head. She fought the urge to throw her third glass bowl at the bathroom door. She just didn't think she could stand much more.

First, that job for Miss Brookner after school. Miss Brookner always counted on her for help. And then her customers. They depended on her to return their fish and turtle bowls on time, in sparkling clean condition. But Belinda was the worst. She expected Jean to jump at all her demands.

If my head would just stop hurting, Jean thought.

Panic seized her, and she attacked the dirt on the turtle bowl. When the last paper towel lay in dirty shreds, she collapsed on the edge of the tub.

Resting her aching head on the cold sink, she tried to calm down. *No one will be terribly upset if I'm a little late,* she told herself sternly. *There's no need to get so upset.* She took several deep breaths.

Jean straightened suddenly and listened. Heavy footsteps on the stairs were followed by a heavy knock on the door. Jean opened the door. "Hi, Dad."

"Aren't you about finished cleaning those bowls? It's nearly six o'clock." He yawned and stretched. "Isn't it your week to cook supper? We're hungry."

"I'm nearly done," Jean said, barely keeping the annoyance out of her voice. When he went downstairs, she shut the door quietly.

Chewing her bottom lip, Jean scraped at the fourth bowl with her fingernail. *Why is everything my fault?* she wondered angrily. *Belinda could have helped with dinner while she waited. That wouldn't have hurt her fingernails.*

Jean's hands shook as she scraped the bowl. It slipped out of her grasp and hit the toothbrushes on the counter. They spilled into the sink.

Sighing, Jean picked up the five brightly colored toothbrushes. As she put them back in the container by the electric toothbrush, an idea slowly formed in her mind. She smiled at her reflection in the mirror.

"Well, they all want me to hurry up." She snapped the blue brush into the electric toothbrush and laughed. "This should work like magic."

Jean squeezed some toothpaste onto the brush. With a whir, the toothbrush began to vibrate. She attacked the dried slime inside the third bowl. Soon the white toothbrush bristles were green and fuzzy-looking.

Jean pulled out the blue brush and snapped in Belinda's red one. She especially enjoyed using *that* one. Soon the bowl gleamed and smelled of mint. Belinda's toothbrush smelled of mildew.

In a few short minutes Jean had used the yellow, green and orange toothbrushes. Rinsing the toothpaste from the fourth bowl, she dried it till it sparkled.

All four bowls were finally clean, just a few minutes past six. All five toothbrushes lay in the sink, green and moldy.

Jean opened the bathroom door and peeked out. She tiptoed as she carried the bowls down to the wagon. At last she was finished. Jean smiled to herself. She knew her family would be shocked when they saw the bathroom.

For once, she thought defiantly, *dependable Jean has done the unexpected.*

10

No More Doormats

As Jean started downstairs with the last clean fishbowl, she saw Belinda come out of their bedroom.

"I'm done now. The bathroom's all yours." Jean
clomped down the stairs.

She heard Belinda get a towel from the hall linen
closet and go into the bathroom. Softly Jean closed
the front door behind her. As she started down the
sidewalk, she heard Belinda's first shriek.

When she was half a block away, her name was
shouted again. Glancing over her shoulder, Jean saw
Belinda standing on the front steps in her bathrobe.

"Jean Harvey, come back here!" she bellowed.
"Come back here right now!"

Pretending not to hear, Jean smiled and quickened her pace. She knew Belinda wouldn't run down the street after her in her robe.

Jean guessed she should feel guilty about what she had just done, but she didn't. She was through taking the blame for things that weren't her fault. She would no longer cover up for her sister. She was finished saying "yes" when she wanted to say "no."

I've had it, she thought. *I've been a doormat for the last time.*

After returning the fish and turtle bowls, Jean turned toward home. Thoughtfully she jingled the change in her pocket. She had walked off much of her anger, and the throbbing in her head had lessened. The pressure of the afternoon had left her exhausted.

Now that she was less angry, the weight of her action began to sink in. The closer she got to home, the slower her feet dragged. She'd almost enjoyed getting back at Belinda. But it wasn't only her sister's toothbrush she'd used to clean the filthy bowls. She'd also used Mark's, although he might not even notice the condition of his toothbrush. But her parents would definitely have something to say about it.

Jean stopped under a tree and sat down in the empty wagon. Now she wondered if being a doormat was really so *bad*. At least she'd never been afraid to go home before.

Jingling her money, Jean knew what she had to do. She rubbed the back of her neck, then rose and turned the wagon around. She plodded four blocks to the local drugstore. Inside she stared at a rack displaying toothbrushes in dazzling colors.

They were thirty-five cents each. Five new toothbrushes would cost most of the two dollars she had just collected. Choosing red, green, orange, blue and yellow toothbrushes from the rack, she paid for them and left. After tax, she had only a nickel and a few pennies left for her afternoon's work.

There must be a better way to declare my independence, Jean thought as she trudged home.

When she walked in the front door, she stopped and sniffed in surprise. The spicy aroma of spaghetti made her mouth water.

Her mother appeared in the kitchen doorway. "I'm glad you're back. I was beginning to wonder what had happened to you." She cocked her head to one side. "What on earth made you use our toothbrushes to clean those dirty fishbowls?"

"I don't know." Jean pulled the five new toothbrushes from her sack. "I bought everybody a new one with the money I collected."

Her mother smiled. "That should help calm Belinda down." She squeezed Jean's shoulder. "Hurry and wash up. We're ready to eat."

Before going to the kitchen, Jean called Stacy and explained that she hadn't eaten yet. "Go ahead swimming without me," she said tiredly. "Have fun."

After Rob picked up Belinda, a welcome calm settled over the house. Jean's parents relaxed in front of an old movie on TV. Mark sprawled on the living room carpet, building a fort out of toy logs.

Jean wandered restlessly around the house. She perched on the arm of a chair in the living room and swung her leg back and forth. "Would you mind if I walked over to Grandma's?" she asked. "I won't stay long."

"That would be nice," her mother mumbled as she munched buttered popcorn. "But be sure you're home before dark."

Strolling down the sidewalk, Jean felt her heart lighten with every block she passed. Maybe no one else understood her, but her grandmother did. Grandma was the only person who liked her just for herself.

Within fifteen minutes Jean was sinking gratefully into her favorite stuffed chair in her grandmother's living room. "What a rotten day this has been," she said. "I felt like I was going crazy."

Her grandmother pulled yellow yarn from a quilted drawstring bag. "What made this day so especially rotten?" she asked as she began crocheting.

At last, Jean thought, someone who cared about *her* feelings. She took a deep breath and began her story. Her voice gradually grew louder and more angry as she recounted how everyone had taken advantage of her. She explained about helping after school, even though she had had to clean the four fish and turtle bowls. She fumed at how often Miss Brookner asked for her help.

Then she confided how Belinda had borrowed her money, promising to pay it back from her baby-sitting jobs, but instead had spent it on Rob. "She had no right to do that," Jean declared.

"I could lend you the money for your puppy," her grandmother interrupted quietly.

Jean shook her head, her lips pressed together. "I couldn't let you do that. I have to earn the money by myself." She continued with her story about Belinda banging on the bathroom door, her parents coming home before supper was ready, and how she'd spent her earnings on new toothbrushes for the whole family.

"I'm sure they expected me to do that," she ended.

Jean took a deep breath and settled deeper into her chair. She was ready to soak up her grandmother's soothing words. She knew she could at least count on her grandmother's sympathy.

"You've had quite a day." Her grandmother continued crocheting on a new afghan. "People do seem to expect a lot from you." She paused and looked directly at Jean. "But it occurs to me that perhaps— just *perhaps*—you like being the only dependable child in the family."

Jean jerked bolt upright. "How can you say that?" She gripped the arms of the chair. "I just told you what a horrible day I had. *That's* what I get for being the girl everyone can count on."

"That's just my point, dear." Her grandmother laid down her yarn. "You must somehow enjoy being the 'girl everyone can count on.' Otherwise you would simply have told your teacher you had a job after school. She would have understood, especially since two other children stayed to help."

"But—"

"I realize it's important to be dependable," she continued, "but no one is indispensable." She shook her head sadly. "Not even you, Jeannie."

"I never said I was indispensable," Jean cried.

"But I'm afraid you act that way. Just think about it." She held up three fingers as she ticked off her reasons. "The schoolroom would have been decorated without your help. Belinda would have been forced to solve her own money problem if you hadn't bailed her out again. And as you pointed out, your mother cooked supper when you were running late. She sounded sympathetic to me."

"Well, yes." Jean felt confused. Her grandmother didn't understand at all. "But—"

"Several times I've offered to watch Mark when Belinda's run out on you. But you never ask me." She patted Jean's clenched fist. "That's why I think you enjoy your reputation as the girl who can always be counted on."

"How can you say that?" Jean's voice rose to a squeak. "It causes me so many problems."

"Yes, it causes problems. But I guess it's a price you're willing to pay." She rose quietly and put away her crocheting.

Jean stood up too. "I have to go," she said stiffly. "I promised to be home before dark." She avoided her grandmother's eyes as she moved to the door.

"Jeannie, wait a minute." Her grandmother turned her around and pulled her close. "Please try to understand why I said those things. I love you. I just want you to be happy." She put a finger under Jean's chin and tilted her face up. "I want you to believe that others like you for yourself, not for the things you are willing to do for them."

Disgusted with herself, Jean felt her eyes fill with tears. "But you don't understand, Grandma. You're the only one who feels that way."

"I guess you'll never know until you try being different." She held the door open for Jean. "If the situation is going to change, it will have to begin with you."

Jean kissed her grandmother and left, deep in thought. She couldn't believe her grandmother had really said all those terrible things to her. She had always trusted that her grandmother understood how things were.

The sky darkened quickly, but Jean was barely aware of her surroundings. Her grandmother's words echoed in her mind. She wished her grandmother were right. She wished others *would* like her, whether or not she did favors for them. Secretly Jean doubted if that were possible.

But one thing was sure. Jean knew she had had all she could take.

Jean mulled over her grandmother's words all weekend. On Sunday night, after Belinda had seemed to avoid her all day, Jean confronted her about the loan. Belinda produced four dollars and fifty cents from her Saturday night's babysitting job and promised to pay more soon. Jean grudgingly decided to give her one more week. She seemed to be serious about paying her back.

On Monday morning Jean joined Stacy on the school steps. "I'm sorry about Friday night," she said. "Did you get to go swimming?"

"Our whole family went," Stacy said. She sucked in her breath sharply. "And guess what? The Six Silver Sharks were practicing for their spring show. Two of them asked me if you were joining me to swim."

"They did? Why?"

"They wanted to talk to you. I'll bet they want to invite you to join their group!"

Jean gripped her hands together to keep from clapping. The Silver Sharks! It was almost too much to hope for. All the dreams she'd dreamed! She could picture herself gliding gracefully through the water, dipping and swaying to the music. . . .

Stacy jolted her out of her daydream. "It's too bad

you couldn't come Friday night. Did Miss Brookner make you late?"

Jean explained about helping decorate the classroom and how she'd rushed to clean her bowls before six o'clock.

"At least you're two dollars closer to bringing your puppy home."

Jean shook her head regretfully and confessed about the toothbrushes.

"Did Belinda at least pay the nine dollars back yesterday? Wasn't that her deadline?"

"She paid me half of it. That's all she had. I'll make sure I get the rest. With the money from cleaning those tanks plus my allowance, I have about twelve dollars. Thank goodness Mr. Sorensen's in no hurry to be paid." They started into the building as the bell rang. "It makes me so mad when I think about her spending my money on Rob."

"You should have known better. Why did you lend her money in the first place? And for pink sandals! You knew you couldn't trust her to keep her promise."

Surprised at her friend's criticism, Jean bit back her retort. She remembered the book Stacy had borrowed but not returned on time. Jean thought she had a lot of nerve to call Belinda unreliable.

Later, Jean sat at her desk, chin in hand. Someday, when she was a poor old woman, people would appreciate her. Her generosity would be known far and wide. Strangers would point to her, knowing she had given all her money to little orphan girls. They would whisper about the hundreds of little girls who, thanks to her, had pink sandals to wear. . . .

She was startled as Jamison tripped "accidentally" over her foot. Jean frowned. Her daydreams didn't help her feel better the way they used to. She just couldn't get her grandmother's words out of her mind. "No one is indispensable," she'd said. "Most of the time people can take care of themselves quite nicely."

Jean felt as if her life was in a mess. Even her grandmother seemed to be against her. Suddenly she knew what would make her feel better—hugging a chubby cocker spaniel puppy. She decided to go out to the Goldridge Animal Shelter right after school.

That afternoon her spirits lifted as she pedaled out to the animal shelter. Arriving out of breath, she parked her bike and hurried inside. Mr. Sorensen stood behind the counter in the reception room.

"Hi, Mr. Sorensen." Jean smiled as he looked up. "I'm surprised to find you in here. Usually I have to ring the little bell on the counter."

He brushed a large hand over his eyes. "I can almost set my watch by you these days. Every Monday at three-forty I can count on Jean Harvey to come through that front door." He held up a sheaf of papers. "I'm addressing a batch of brochures. If I do this in my office, I can't hear the bell."

"Have you cleaned the cat cages yet?" Jean asked.

"No, but don't worry about that. I'll get around to it pretty soon."

"That's okay. I don't mind." Jean moved through the door behind the counter.

Mr. Sorensen called after her. "I'm afraid you've gotten stuck with this on all your visits here."

"But I enjoy doing it." Jean laughed at his skeptical expression. "Honest." She began tearing old newspapers into strips.

Mr. Sorensen hesitated, then followed her into the cat room. "I hate to bring this up after all the help you've been."

Jean frowned when Mr. Sorensen wouldn't meet her eyes. "What is it?" she asked.

"It's about Marshmallow. I know I told you four weeks ago that you didn't have to pay for her right away." He rubbed his inky fingers up and down his pants leg. "But something's come up."

Jean could scarcely breathe. "What's happened?"

"A woman came here Saturday. She saw Marshmallow and wanted to take her right away." He spread his huge hands wide. "I explained that someone else wanted her. She asked if the fee was paid. I had to say no."

"What are you trying to say?"

"We don't really have a policy for saving dogs for people. I shouldn't have told you that. It's just so rare for two people to want the same animal. The woman wants to replace her daughter's tan cocker puppy that was hit by a car." He looked at her hopefully. "You said it would take only a few weeks to save the fifteen dollars. Could you possibly pay for her this week? Then, when the lady checks back, I can say she's been taken home."

Jean mentally counted her money. With what Belinda had repaid, she had had a little more than twelve dollars. But she'd needed a new notebook last week and had also spent three dollars on a birthday gift for Mark. That left about seven dollars. Only half of what she needed!

"Some things have happened in the last two weeks—expenses that I hadn't counted on," Jean said, remembering Belinda's loan and all those toothbrushes. "Could I make a deposit on Marshmallow?"

"I usually don't take deposits. It just makes extra paperwork." He pulled on the corner of his lip. "Tell you what I'll do. I'll give you another week. I'll stall the lady that long. But I'm afraid I'll need the money then or I'll have to let her have Marshmallow."

Jean swallowed hard, but the lump in her throat remained. "Thank you, Mr. Sorensen. I'll see what I can do. I honestly thought I would have the money before now."

Nodding, Mr. Sorensen went back to mailing out brochures. Almost in a trance, Jean cleaned the cat cages. She had become quite skillful at the job and had no trouble with runaway cats. In half an hour she had finished. Walking down the hall to the dog cages in the back room, she laid her plans.

Catching sight of her, Marshmallow wiggled over to the door of the cage. She looked up with a curious expression, as if asking why Jean didn't let her out to play.

Leaning against the cage door, Jean spoke softly. "Hi there, girl. It looks like we've got a big problem to solve." She knelt down and reached her fingers through the wire. "I'll come up with something. I have to."

Jean rubbed behind Marshmallow's ear. "I know Mr. Sorensen can't help it. It's really my own fault. That's what I get for fixing everyone else's problems instead of working on my own."

Marshmallow cocked her head to one side, as if listening to Jean. "But I won't lose you because of it." Jean spoke with determination. "I'm going to look out for myself from now on—and let other people solve their own problems."

Standing up, Jean squared her thin shoulders. People might not see it yet, but she had changed. She was through being walked on. She intended to erase those footprints up her back.

In short, Jean planned to revolt.

11

Revolt

The next morning Jean awoke early with fresh determination. She had promised herself that things were going to change. Swinging her legs over the side of the bed, she decided there was no time like the present to begin.

Tiptoeing around the room, Jean dressed for school without waking Belinda. She wanted to eat early and finish studying for her history test before leaving for school.

She looked in disgust at the condition of their room. Clothes were draped over chairs and strewn across the floor. Books and papers were stacked in tilting piles under the window. Towels from last night's baths hung on doorknobs and bedposts.

Jean grabbed her dirty clothes and towel, throwing them in the hamper. Then she made her bed and picked up her books. She surveyed the room. At least her half of the bedroom was clean.

At the door she paused and turned around. Picking up her own things hadn't helped a bit, she decided. The room still looked like a wreck. Jean knew Belinda's clothes wouldn't get picked up unless their mother happened to see the clutter.

Jean started back into the room. It would only take a minute to pick up Belinda's junk. She wasn't really doing it for her sister. Jean simply hated coming home to a messy room after school.

Bending over to pick up Belinda's jogging shoes, Jean stopped with one shoe in her hand. She had totally forgotten. Today was the day she would let Belinda start taking care of her own problems. She dropped the shoe next to its mate and started down to the kitchen.

After bolting down her toast and orange juice, Jean kissed her parents as they left for work. Her mother called up the stairs to Belinda before going out the front door.

Jean frowned with concentration. The names of the Civil War battles were so confusing. She barely looked up when Belinda shuffled into the kitchen, still in her pajamas.

Belinda yawned loudly and stretched gracefully, like a cat.

"Are you just now getting up?" Jean asked.

"I guess I forgot to set my alarm." Belinda dropped two slices of bread into the toaster. "Are you finished eating?"

"Yes, quite a while ago," Jean said, returning to her book.

"Good. I have something for you to do." Belinda held up a wrinkled blouse. "I want you to iron this for me while I eat. If you do, I just might make it to school on time." Belinda plugged in the iron and dropped the blouse on the ironing board.

Jean watched, aware of a growing resentment. Remembering her intentions, she took a deep breath. "I can't do it. I'm studying for a test this morning."

Belinda raised a perfectly shaped eyebrow at her. "But if you don't, I'll be late for school." Her lower lip protruded slightly.

"I guess you'll have to be late." Jean bent over her book. She refused to look at Belinda's fluttering eyelashes and downcast face.

"But I won't have time to eat," she protested. Her toast popped up from the toaster. "You know how I suffer from migraines when I don't eat on time." Her feeble voice hinted that she was on the verge of fainting from hunger already.

"I'm sorry." Jean covered her ears. "But that's your problem."

"What's come over you this morning?" Belinda snapped. She took a bite from her toast and grabbed the iron. Mumbling through a mouthful of toast about hardhearted sisters, she pressed her blouse.

Jean heard every muffled word, but pretended not to.

"Oh, drat it!" Belinda slammed down the iron and glared at Jean. "Now look what you made me do! I've got a butter stain on my blouse."

Out of the corner of her eye, Jean watched her scrub the stain. After finishing the ironing, Belinda rushed upstairs to get dressed. Jean glanced at the clock. Even if Belinda ran all the way, she would still be late.

Jean sighed and closed her book. Noticing Belinda's uneaten breakfast made her feel ashamed. *But why should I feel guilty?* she thought. It wasn't her fault her sister hadn't set the alarm. Belinda could have ironed her blouse the night before too. Anyway, she *had* needed to do some last minute studying for her test.

Jean nodded firmly. She knew she had done the right thing.

Even so, pangs of guilt bothered her all morning. Although she concentrated on her schoolwork, an uneasy feeling stayed in the back of her mind. Rebelling was harder than she had expected.

After lunch Jean and Stacy were talking outside when a group of girls approached them. Jean's breathing quickened. These girls were the Six Silver Sharks!

Nancy McLinden, the head shark, stepped to the

front of the group. "We wondered if we could speak to Jean." Her eyes flicked briefly to Stacy. "Alone, please."

Stacy backed away. "Um, sure. I'll be by the door when you're done, Jean." She smiled uncertainly and left.

Jean stood very still, trying not to appear too excited. Could this be what she hoped it was? She was almost afraid to speak. The Silver Sharks wouldn't want her in their group if she babbled like a baby.

Linda Jorgensen laid an arm on Jean's sleeve. "We've watched you swimming at the Y during the winter. We're all impressed with your style."

Jean felt her face grow warm under their stares. "Thank you. I've always liked to swim." She imagined herself already in a swimsuit with a fin on her back.

"We have our spring show at the Y in May. It's only a few weeks away," Nancy explained. "You've seen us perform, I assume." She spoke matter-of-factly, as if she couldn't imagine anyone not having seen their show.

Jean nodded, too excited to speak.

"What we want is this. We need publicity for our show. We liked the posters you did for the class bake sale before Christmas," she said.

Jean stared at the girls for a minute without blinking. Then she swallowed hard, trying to hide her disappointment. "You mean you want me to make posters advertising your May show?" She was glad her voice didn't shake. She hoped they couldn't tell her knees did.

"That's right," Linda said in a breezy tone. "We felt we could count on you to have the posters done on time—"

"—and displayed in the proper places," Nancy added.

Jean scuffed her foot back and forth in the gravel. "Well . . . I'm really very busy these days. I have a job after school."

Nancy interrupted her, her eyes opened wide. "Perhaps you don't understand. It's true that you wouldn't swim in the May show. But doing us this little kindness would be in your favor when we decide to add someone to our group. That *could* be very soon."

Suddenly Jean was furious. She knew a bribe when she heard one. After all, Belinda had offered enough of them. She was positive that the Sharks had no intention of ever asking her to join their swimming group.

Stiffening her knocking knees, she spoke slowly. "I'd appreciate your considering me when you add to your group." She kept her voice level. "But I really can't do the posters for you. I have too many things to do already. Good luck with your May show." Her heart pounding, she turned and walked away.

But she saw the angry look that passed between

Nancy and Linda. Jean would be surprised if any of the Sharks spoke to her for a long time. Without a doubt, she could kiss her dream of swimming with the Silver Sharks good-bye.

She joined Stacy and explained what had happened. "So much for ever swimming under colored lights," she ended.

Stacy frowned slightly. "Do you think that was such a good idea? Maybe they *were* going to invite you to join their group."

Shuffling into the building, Jean mulled over Stacy's words. Had she done something dumb? Was she overdoing this rebellion thing? *Had* she blown her only chance to join that "in" group?

It was a long afternoon. In gym Jean ended up on the same volleyball team as three of the Silver Sharks. They avoided speaking to her and refused to help her return any balls. Jean knew by the heat radiating from her face that she was blushing six shades of red.

She told Stacy about it as they walked home after school. Stacy understood. She had seen what happened during gym class.

Abruptly Stacy stopped. "Oh, no! I forgot my science notes. And I need them for that experiment we have to do tonight."

"Are you going back to get them?"

"I can't. I'm late for my route already." She shook her fuzzy pigtails. "Let me borrow your notes. I could use them after my route while you clean that fishtank today. Then I'll bring the notes to your house. You can do the experiment after supper." She held her hand out.

Jean hesitated, staring down at the sidewalk.

"What's the matter?" Stacy asked. "You remembered your science notes, didn't you?"

"Yes, but . . ."

"But what?"

"Remember the last time you borrowed a book to study for a test and promised to bring it back?" she asked. "You never showed up. I didn't do very well on that test."

"I couldn't help that!" Stacy protested. "My dad was mad and grounded me." She folded her arms across her chest.

"I have an idea," Jean said. "Why don't you come over after supper and we could do the experiment together?"

Stacy's eyes narrowed. "In other words, you won't let me borrow your notes?" Her tone was cutting. "I always thought I could count on you, Jean."

"You're the one who warned me not to lend things to people who aren't dependable." She hugged her books tight.

"Excuse me!" Stacy pivoted on her heel and stalked down the street.

"Wait a minute!" Jean called, starting after her.

Stacy began running. Jean gave up following her

and headed home. Her stomach churned as she remembered Stacy's words: "I thought I could count on you."

Was she being hasty? Jean wondered. Shouldn't friends be able to count on each other? Was her revolt going too far?

Jean sighed inwardly. She wasn't at all sure she liked being independent. What if she found out that people only liked her for the things she did for them? Did she want to take that chance?

Trudging along, Jean felt so alone. She wondered if she were giving up too much for her independence. She didn't seem to be getting much in return.

•

12

Puppy Paw Prints

The next afternoon at school Jean worked at a table with four other students. She patted and shaped her gooey plaster. For social studies her group was making a relief map of the United States. Standing back, Jean tried to see if her lumps and peaks looked at all like the Rocky Mountains.

Jamison had scooped out five depressions in his section of map. "How do you like the Great Lakes?" he asked.

Stacy snickered. "Looks more like a dog with droopy ears," she whispered to Jean. Stacy had apologized to Jean that morning about their argument. Jean had been surprised, but relieved.

Miss Brookner came up behind them. "I think

that looks very nice, Jami." She examined their map. "Perhaps Lake Superior could be a little bigger."

"I still think it looks like a pint-sized dog," Stacy said, laughing.

"Maybe *your* dog, but not mine. I have a huge collie." Jami dug one lake a little deeper. "But he's no fun anymore."

"Why not?" Miss Brookner asked.

"He won't run or play catch with me, or anything. He just lies around all the time." Jami flung a piece of wet plaster at Stacy. "And he drools worse than my baby brother."

Jean glanced up sharply, remembering the dog at the animal shelter. "You should have him checked for rabies," she said.

"Rabies? You're nuts!" Jamison rolled his eyes. "He's not racing around crazy and foaming at the mouth."

"That's a common mistake, thinking an animal with rabies has to act like that." Jean added one more peak to her mountain chain. "Rabies is caught through an animal's saliva when he bites you. An exhausted animal that drools a lot could have rabies."

Miss Brookner was widening Lake Superior. She stopped with one finger stuck in the plaster. "How do you know this?"

"A vet at the Goldridge Animal Shelter told me." Jean wiped her hands on a paper towel. "They thought one of the dogs had rabies. He was very sleepy, and drooled some too. He didn't have rabies, it turned out. But the vet said he had the right symptoms."

"Do you have a pet from the animal shelter?" her teacher asked.

"I will soon. I'm saving my money for a puppy." Jean warmed to her favorite topic. "I go there every week to visit her."

"My sister should visit that place," Jami said. "She wants a kitten for her birthday."

"They have some cats there as well as dogs," Jean said. "They want to get most of them adopted. A few animals are just staying there while their owners are on vacation."

"You say you're saving money for a puppy?" Miss Brookner frowned. "I thought the stray animals were free."

"They aren't free." Jean shook her head. "The money you pay goes for food, and later for shots, if you take home a puppy or a kitten. Mr. Sorensen— he runs the animal shelter—really feels bad about the stray animals that don't get homes."

Miss Brookner scraped a pile of plaster from the floor and threw it in the wastebasket. "That sounds like an interesting place for the class to visit."

Stacy spoke eagerly. "Jean talks about the shelter all the time. Couldn't we go there for a field trip?"

Miss Brookner glanced questioningly at Jean. "Well . . ."

Jean nodded. "Would you like me to ask Mr. Sorensen if our class can visit the shelter? I'm sure he wouldn't mind showing us around and telling us about his job."

"Do you think so?" Miss Brookner tapped her finger on her chin. "I guess you could go ahead and ask him. If Mr. Sorensen agrees, have him call me here at school. Then we can choose a day to go."

Jami picked the plaster from the front of his T-shirt. "That would be a neat trip! Maybe we could play with the animals. That's lots better than visiting that dumb clock factory."

Jean had to agree, even with Jamison. As she washed at the sink, she was aware of a new warm feeling inside. Maybe Grandma was right. Maybe others *would* like her for herself and find her interesting.

Jean had promised to watch Mark that afternoon, so she hurried home right after school. She was surprised to find Belinda there, mixing something in the kitchen. Her older sister hadn't spoken to her since the morning before when she'd refused to iron her blouse. So Jean quickly grabbed two apples and headed back towards the living room.

"Jean? Wait a minute." Belinda wiped her hands on a dishtowel.

Jean bit into her crunchy Jonathan apple. "What do you want?" She braced herself for a lecture.

"I just wanted to tell you that since I was home this afternoon, I'd watch Mark and you could spend some time with Stacy." She motioned toward the mixing bowl. "I'm making pizza for supper."

Jean's eyes narrowed. "You're willing to watch Mark *and* fix supper for me?" She sighed aloud. "What do you want this time? You must know I won't lend you any more money."

Belinda ran her fingers through her hair. "I can see why you'd think that. But honestly—I don't want anything."

Jean waited, munching quietly. She couldn't pin it down, but there was something new about Belinda. She almost believed her sister.

Belinda continued stirring the pizza dough. "I've been thinking. I guess I have taken advantage of you lately and expected you to cover for me a lot." She paused and glanced at Jean. "I haven't always been very fair, and I'm sorry."

Jean stared for several seconds at her older sister. "That's all right," she said. Surprisingly, she realized she meant it. "Really it is."

Belinda smiled suddenly. "Thanks. Now don't you have something you want to do while I fix supper? My new generous mood is bound to pass before long. Enjoy it while it lasts."

Jean grinned and backed out the door, remembering the phone call she wanted to make. She couldn't wait to ask Mr. Sorensen about the possibility of a class trip. Upstairs, she called him and explained about her talk with Miss Brookner. He quickly assured her that her class was welcome.

"Which day next week did you have in mind?" Mr. Sorensen asked.

Jean was eager to show Stacy her puppy. "Would Monday morning be too soon?"

Mr. Sorensen laughed. "That would be fine. You said I should call your teacher at school?"

"Yes. She has to arrange to use the school bus for the trip."

"Okay, I'll call her first thing tomorrow morning." Mr. Sorensen paused. "I hate to bring up an unpleasant topic, but I'm afraid I have to. The lady who wants to adopt Marshmallow was here again today. I have to give her an answer soon."

Jean's stomach flipflopped. She did some quick mental addition. She had seven dollars in her tin box. To that she added what she would earn from cleaning Mrs. Thompkins's tank on Thursday and the four bowls on Friday, plus her allowance on Saturday. If Belinda repaid at least two more dollars, she should have enough.

"I'll bring the money on Monday. Please give me until then." Jean twisted the telephone cord around her finger.

"Monday should be soon enough. I think Marshmallow will be glad to go home with you. And I'm looking forward to having your class visit. Maybe some of your friends will be in the market for a pet."

"I hope so, Mr. Sorensen. Thank you for letting us come. I'll pay you the fifteen dollars for Marshmallow on Monday." She spoke with more confidence than she felt. She said good-bye, hung up and collapsed into the chair by the phone.

Doodling on the note pad by the phone, Jean hoped she were right. She simply *had* to have the money by Monday.

Suddenly she hit her forehead with the palm of her hand. Before she brought Marshmallow home, she would have to buy some puppy food and a collar. Jean's thoughts whirled. Belinda would just have to find a way to pay off the rest of her loan. And it had to be soon. Otherwise Jean wouldn't be able to pay for Marshmallow and that other lady would take her home. Jean wouldn't allow that to happen.

By Monday morning, Jean had collected the money for cleaning the tank and bowls. Added to her allowance, she had slightly over thirteen dollars. Unfortunately, Belinda didn't babysit over the weekend and could repay nothing on her loan. That left Jean still two dollars short.

Jean couldn't wait for their field trip that morning. She was anxious to tell Mr. Sorensen she had most of the money. Her mother hadn't let her bring thirteen dollars to school. She would have to go home for it after school to make a deposit on Marshmallow. Surely thirteen dollars would be enough for a deposit. Then Mr. Sorensen could tell the lady to choose another puppy for her daughter.

On the bus that morning Miss Brookner sat with

Jean, asking her questions about the animal shelter. Jean felt very important. She tried to remember the interesting things Mr. Sorensen and Brent Davis had told her. She was eager to introduce Mr. Sorensen to her class. She hoped they liked him as much as she did.

When they arrived Jean was pleased to see Mr. Sorensen holding open the front door. The students surged inside. Mr. Sorensen patted Jean's shoulder as she was swept past him.

"I know it's crowded in the waiting area, but I think you can all squeeze in." He waved his big hand to get their attention. "I'm Mr. Sorensen. I manage things here at the Goldridge Animal Shelter. We'll take a short tour first. Then, if your teacher permits, I'll let you play with some of the animals. Maybe, if I'm lucky, a few of you will see animals that you'd like to take home." He smiled and raised his voice. "Feel free to ask questions as we go along."

He pressed through the students to the door behind the counter. "If you'll follow me . . ."

They crowded into the middle room where the cages held cats of various sizes and colors. Melanie and Nancy oohed and aahed over the latest litter of striped kittens. Jamison poked his finger through the tabby's cage, where the hissing cat promptly scratched him.

Mr. Sorensen pointed to the cages. "Here we keep our cats and other small animals. Sometimes we have rabbits and hamsters, but at this time it's mostly kittens." He opened a cage and held up a sleek black tom cat. "The animals with blue tags on their cages are not for sale. They stay here while their owners are on vacation. We make money to run the shelter by boarding animals like a kennel."

"Where do you get the animals that you put up for adoption?" Stacy asked, balancing on her tiptoes to see over Stuart.

Mr. Sorensen rubbed his hand over his bald head. "Sometimes owners bring in a new litter of kittens they don't want. In that case the owners pay for enough food to last a month. Usually we find homes for the kittens by that time." He opened another cage and gently held up one of the new striped kittens. "But some of the animals are strays. People find them wandering around and bring them to us. If they're not wearing ID tags, we advertise the animals for two weeks. If no one claims them, then they're put up for adoption."

Jami waved his hand wildly. "Last year my dad found a dog that was hit by a car. I think he brought it here."

Mr. Sorensen nodded. "He might have. Sometimes we get injured strays. When that happens, I call this man." He pointed to the door behind them.

As if on cue, the students turned around together. Brent Davis stood in the doorway.

Mr. Sorensen motioned for him to join them.

"This is Brent Davis, the veterinarian I call most often. He donates his time to come out to the animal shelter."

Jean opened her eyes wide. She hadn't known that. Her opinion of Brent Davis rose several points.

For several minutes Brent answered questions about his job. He said that most of his work was taking care of animals. He worked at an animal hospital, where he treated sick animals or ones that had been in accidents. He explained that some vets, however, ran pet stores, checked dairy herds or did animal research.

When he began talking about safety and health care for pets, Jean grew impatient. She wanted to move to the dog room and show Marshmallow to her friends.

She was also anxious to speak privately to Mr. Sorensen. She wanted to tell him about the money she would bring after school. She clasped her fingers in a tight grip. She hoped desperately that he would bend the rules and take a deposit on Marshmallow. If not, she intended to ask her grandmother for a small loan but only as a last resort.

At last it was time to move to the dog room. Jean and the other students followed Mr. Sorensen down the long hall that connected the rooms. Jean was near the back of the group and couldn't see the dogs at first. Barking and yipping filled the air. Mr. Sorensen didn't try to talk until the yapping subsided.

"As you can see, this is where we keep the dogs and puppies." He pointed to the rear of the cage. "There is a small door back there to let the dog pass through to an outside pen. Fresh air and exercise are very important for the dogs." He started down the rows of cages as he talked.

Stuart pointed to a half-grown terrier he spotted. "Could I sign up for that dog?"

Mr. Sorensen shook his head. "I'm afraid our rule is that you must pay the fee first. We have to let the people with enough money adopt the dogs. I wish it were different. We just can't afford to 'save' an animal for anyone."

Stacy whispered to Jean. "I thought he was saving Marshmallow for you."

"Not really." Jean wrapped a strand of hair around her finger. "Until last week, no one else wanted her. But now a lady wants to buy her. Mr. Sorensen said I have to pay for Marshmallow this week. Otherwise he'll have to let the woman take her home."

Stacy's eyes opened wide. "You don't have the fifteen dollars yet, do you?"

"No, just thirteen dollars. But I'm going to ask him again if I can make a deposit. I just can't let someone else have my puppy!"

"Where is Marshmallow, anyway?" Stacy stood on tiptoe and peered over the shoulders of the others. "I don't see her."

Jean pointed eagerly toward the end of the row of cages. "She's down there. She's in a cage with a few brothers and sisters and her mother. You'll love her." Jean zigzagged through the group of students. "Follow me. She's the cutest—" She stopped abruptly, her sentence cut off.

Stacy bumped into her. "What's the matter?"

Jean stared into Marshmallow's cage. She refused to believe her eyes. Three of Marshmallow's brothers and sisters romped around the cage, tumbling over each other. But no plump tan puppy was there. Jean hurried to a nearby window. Maybe Marshmallow had gone outside through the small swinging door. But the tiny pen outside was empty.

Jean leaned against the wall. Her knees threatened to buckle.

She couldn't believe it. Marshmallow wasn't there. Had Mr. Sorensen been trying to warn her a while ago? Was he talking about Marshmallow when he told Stuart he couldn't save animals for anyone? Had the lady with fifteen dollars already taken her home?

With a sick feeling in the pit of her stomach, Jean knew she was too late. Somewhere in Goldridge, Marshmallow was living with another family. Remembering the doghouse and dish waiting at home, Jean had to fight to hold back the tears.

She turned to Stacy, wiping her hand across her eyes. "It looks like I'm too late. Marshmallow's been taken." She searched the crowd for Mr. Sorensen. She had to talk to him.

She spotted him, but he was surrounded by kids

asking questions. Then he opened several cages. While the students played with the dogs, Mr. Sorensen talked to Brent and Miss Brookner.

Feeling miserable, Jean watched other puppies frolicking on the floor with the kids from her class. She knew that soon she could afford to buy another puppy. She narrowed her eyes. None of the puppies she saw compared to Marshmallow. She couldn't imagine another puppy in her yellow doghouse. If she couldn't have Marshmallow, Jean thought, she didn't want a puppy at all.

It took five minutes of chasing puppies to get them sorted out and back in their cages. Then Miss Brookner motioned for the class to follow Mr. Sorensen. Laughing and pushing good-naturedly, they went back down the long hall, past the closed office door, and into the waiting room.

Jean plodded slowly at the end of the line. Now she was afraid to ask Mr. Sorensen about Marshmallow. She couldn't stand to hear him say the awful words.

In the waiting room the students milled around, talking and laughing.

Mr. Sorensen motioned them quiet. "I'm glad you all could come. Before you go, I have an announcement." The students turned toward him. "Jean, could you come up here a minute?"

Jean's eyes opened wide in surprise. Stacy nudged her forward. Slowly Jean worked her way through the crowd to stand near Mr. Sorensen by the long counter. Mr. Sorensen put a large hand on her shoulder.

"First I want to thank Jean for arranging to have you come out today."

Shouts and shrill whistles filled the air. Jean tried to smile, but her lips felt frozen.

"Jean and I met nearly six weeks ago when she came to look at puppies," Mr. Sorensen continued. "She's been working and saving for a tan cocker spaniel. Every week she's come to visit the puppy. But Jean's done something else every week too."

Jean noticed curious looks pass between her classmates. She wondered what Mr. Sorensen was leading up to.

"Jean spent much of her time, not playing with her puppy, but cleaning cages and feeding cats for me." He smiled at her. "I could count on her help every Monday afternoon. And I'm sure I can depend on her to give Marshmallow a good home."

Jean glanced up quickly. What was Mr. Sorensen saying?

Then, a movement at the door behind the counter caught her eye. A short yip came from the cage that Brent Davis carried. The vet set the cage on the counter. Marshmallow stared at Jean with big brown eyes. Jean's mouth fell open as she stared at the puppy.

Mr. Sorensen grinned at her surprise. "I knew Jean was planning to take Marshmallow home this week. We thought it would be nice for her to take her puppy home this morning. Marshmallow has been waiting in this cage in my office."

Jean opened her mouth and closed it several times, but no words came out.

Mr. Sorensen turned to Miss Brookner. "If it's okay with your teacher, you can take the puppy home now on the bus. You've been waiting a long time for this day."

Miss Brookner frowned, then slowly smiled at Jean. "I guess it would be all right. It'll be lunchtime when we get back to school. You can take her home then if you'd like."

"But Mr. Sorensen—" Jean's words were drowned out by the cheering of her friends. Jean was jostled as the students pushed toward the counter to see Marshmallow. Then Miss Brookner herded them out to the bus. Jean hung back.

When the room had cleared, she turned to Mr. Sorensen. "This was so nice of you, but I have a problem."

Mr. Sorensen crouched down beside her, placing the cage on the floor. "What is it?"

"I know I told you I could pay the fifteen dollars today. I really tried, but I'm still a little short." She chewed on her bottom lip. "I can't take Marshmallow home after all." Her voice faded to barely more than a whisper.

To Jean's surprise, Mr. Sorensen grinned at her. "Do you have ten dollars?" he asked.

"Ten dollars?" Jean was puzzled. "Yes. In fact, I

have a little over thirteen dollars. But that isn't enough."

"As it turns out, it is." Mr. Sorensen opened the cage and scratched Marshmallow behind her ear. He picked her up and handed the squirming puppy to Jean. "I talked to the owner of the shelter. I explained about the five weeks you helped me here. He said I couldn't pay you for helping, but I could certainly take a little off the fee for the puppy. Mr. Jacobs, the owner, thought ten dollars was a fair amount."

Jean squeezed her puppy tightly. "I can't believe it! Thank you!" Without thinking, she hugged Mr. Sorensen with one arm while holding Marshmallow with the other. "I'll come out right after school. I'll pay the ten dollars then and bring this cage back. I just can't believe it!"

"You deserve it," Mr. Sorensen said.

"I'd better go now." Jean replaced her puppy in the cage. Carrying it to the door, she turned and paused. "Anytime you need someone to clean cages, you just call me. I'll come right over." She smiled, pushed open the door with her back and left.

Her class erupted into applause as Jean boarded the steps of the bus. Miss Brookner had saved the front seat for her, and Jean shared it with Marshmallow. She poked her fingers through the cage, trying to pet her. Marshmallow licked her fingers twice, then settled down for the ride, her head on her paws.

Conversation flowed around her, but Jean was lost in thought. She still couldn't believe that Marshmallow was hers to keep. She had been so sure she'd lost her.

But Mr. Sorensen had said he could depend on her to give Marshmallow a good home. There *were* some good things about being dependable after all. Jean decided she didn't have to change as drastically as she'd feared. She never wanted to be a slave again, that was for sure. But she knew she didn't have to let people walk on her anymore.

Opening the cage, she let Marshmallow crawl out and into her lap. Holding her close, Jean buried her face in the puppy's tan fur. Marshmallow wiggled around and licked the end of Jean's nose.

Being honest with herself, Jean knew her new independence didn't apply to Marshmallow. She would do lots of things for her puppy—bathe her often, brush her fur, put a curtain over the doghouse door, bring her special bones from the butcher. . . . She'd gladly do anything to make Marshmallow feel happy and loved.

Laughing, Jean decided her life might not be so different after all. She was still going to be walked on. She was just trading the human footprints up her back for tracks of puppy paws.

And she didn't mind one bit.